CROW

Soulless Bastards MC
So Cal

Crow

Soulless Bastards MC

So Cal

By Erin Trejo

Edited by: Elfwerks Editing

Proofreader: Chriss Prokic

Cover Design: Nicole Blanchard with
IndieSage PR

Cover Model: Dean McCudden

Contents

A special thank you!

Without my amazing readers I would be nothing. You guys mean the world to me. I just wanted to let you know that. I know I don't always add things in the front of my books like I should but I love you guys!!!

The super special thank you goes to Bink Cummings. There was an integral part of this book that was just killing me. I couldn't figure out what was off about it. So, I asked her and she hooked a bitch up! LOL Bink, I can't thank you enough for helping me out with that part. It means the world to me that you would even help me! You rock! If you haven't checked out Bink's books, you are missing out!

I also need to shout out to Dean McCudden for allowing me to use the most amazing photo of him as the cover for Crow. I think it captures his character perfectly! You rock, Dean! <3

Chapter 1

Four minutes. Four painstaking minutes of my life. It sounds like nothing. To some, it may be, but for me four minutes was all it took to ruin my life. That's all it took to steal the breath from my body.

I shake my head as I sit in the darkness of the warehouse, a bottle of whiskey in my hand. Tears prickle my eyes, the gun rests heavily and tauntingly in my other hand. But that's not what holds my interests. It's the girl. She sits in the middle of the room, not far from me. She can't see me in the shadows. She can't see the monster that sits only a few feet away from her. She takes a long pull from the bottle she has in her hand. The moonlight filtering in through the busted window casting shadows over her face. She holds a razor blade in her hand. She twists and turns it, watching the blade flicker with the light.

"You're too fat," she says to herself, sliding the blade along the skin on her arm. I watch as if I'm in a trance, not wanting to break her moment. "You're disgusting. You're ugly. You aren't worth anything. Why can't you be normal? Why do you have to be you?" Words leave her mouth and with each one, she drags the blade over a new spot on her arm until it's completely covered in her blood. I chuckle lightly, startling her. She looks up, her eyes trying to pick me out of the darkness.

"Wrist to elbow," I finally say. The girl scrambles back, her blade falling to the dirty floor. I scoot out of my spot in the corner and sit my gun on the ground next to me. Her eyes follow my movements but she doesn't say a word. I pick up the blade and hold it in my fingers, her blood now coating my skin and say, "Wrist to elbow." I drag the blade over my skin to demonstrate for her but not enough to draw blood.

"Who are you?" she asks, scooting closer to me. I watch her as she moves, cocking my head to the side. She isn't afraid of me or maybe she's too drunk to give a damn.

"Crow," is all I say.

She looks at the gun and the bottle of whiskey before she moves even closer. "Same idea?" she asks, nodding toward the gun.

My eyes still feel heavy and my brain is not functioning right. I don't know what I'm doing here anymore. "Depends. What are you doin'?" I ask her.

When she scoots into the light once more, I see her. It's not her size that calls to me, it's her eyes and those fucking pouty lips. She's bigger than girls I've messed with. I can see the slight bulge that is her body as she sits there. None of that means shit to me. She shifts uncomfortably as I take her in.

"You ever hate your life so much that you want it to end, Crow?" she asks, pain lacing her voice. I nod my head.

"Every day. Every day of my life," I say truthfully as I pass the blade to her and pick up the gun. I scratch the side of my head with it as memories assault me. Those eyes. That smile. It's all more than any one man should have to bear in his lifetime.

"It'll make it all go away. All the pain. All the names. Everything," she says, pulling my attention back to her. I cock my head and look at her eyes. The key to the soul is always the eyes. Most don't look. Most just think they know a person and know what they feel but they don't. When you look into their eyes, you will see it. You will see all the pain and torment that they have faced. Her gaze slowly slides to the floor in front of us.

"Does it, though? Will it ever go away? Can it?" I ask her.

She looks up, her eyes finding mine in the moonlight. She's gorgeous. She's beautiful. Her life has to have some kind of meaning to it.

"Yeah. It does. When we can't feel anymore. When we can't be hurt anymore. It does," she says softly. I take another pull as I let that sink in.

"Do you know how long it takes someone to die by strangulation?" I ask, my voice catching.

"No."

"Up to one minute. One minute, yeah?" I ask.

She looks at me strangely before she asks, "Who was it?" I shake my head not wanting to answer that.

"That motherfucker who did it took four. Four minutes." I nod as my eyes fill further with unshed tears. "Can you even imagine bein' so close to death only to be pulled back and start all over again?" My voice is hoarse as the tears finally fall. I don't give a shit. She doesn't know me. She doesn't see the real me. So, I let them fall.

"That had to be horrible," she says softly. Her hand comes to mine, her fingers curling around it. I stare at our intertwined hands. A woman I don't even know trying to comfort me. What a fucking joke.

"Yeah, well." I sniff as I pull my hand free and wipe my face. "What are you doin' here?" I ask her.

"I'm tired of being told I'm not good enough. I'm tired of being told that I'm too fat to find love. I'm too ugly to get a man. Do you know what it feels like to hear those words every day of your life?" she asks then looks at me again. "Of course, you wouldn't," she says after taking me in.

"Don't do that. You don't know me," I snap at her. She laughs and it's the most beautiful yet horrifying sound I've ever heard.

"You don't look like me! Look at you!" She waves her hand up and down to make her point. "I'm still a virgin! I'm freaking twenty-two and still a virgin. Do you know why?" She leans closer, looking me in the eye. She's clearly drunk but so the fuck am I.

"No."

"Because I'm too fat to be fucked! I've heard it. Over and over. Maybe if you lose some weight you could find a man. Molested? Oh, I've been that. I was good enough for that, but to actually have a man? A real man who wanted me?

Nope. Never." The tears that clogged her throat now roll down her cheeks as I set my bottle on the ground next to me. I shove the gun up next to it before I move.

Chapter 2

I squat in front of her, our eyes staying glued to each other. There it is. The hesitation that I knew would be there. She's afraid of me, of what I might do to her.

"There are many things I've learned over my lifetime. People are nothin'. In the end, they mean nothin'. No one can tell you what you are except you. You're beautiful. If they couldn't see that, that's their problem, darlin' not yours. Don't let some bastard tell you you aren't good enough." She stares into my eyes and I want to reach out and comfort her but who the fuck am I? I'm no better than the motherfuckers I'm telling her about. In fact, I may just be worse.

"Look at you. You wouldn't understand. People like you walk around with their perfect bodies and have shit handed to them. People like me are the ones in the corners cowering in fear of others. Always the outsiders. Always the weird or disgusting ones. You wouldn't know shit." Her voice drops as she looks down at her blade. I reach for it, taking it between my fingers. I flip it around a few times before I reach for her arm. She doesn't stop me and it makes me wonder why. Why let someone you don't even know touch you like this? Why let them hold your life in their hands?

"When you close your eyes, you feel it. You feel what others can do to you. Whether you let them or not," I tell her. I press the blade against her skin before looking into her eyes. "Close your eyes, sweetheart." Much to my surprise, she does it. Her blue eyes slowly fall closed, her wet lashes brushing against her cheeks. I look back at my hand, the one with the blade before slowly dragging it over her skin. The blood rushes to the surface, but what hypnotizes me? She gasped. Not a scared or a hurt gasp. A sexual gasp. She likes the pain.

I look at the blood as it flows from her skin, wondering what's running through her head but at the same time not caring. I came here to finish my life. I came here to make the nightmares stop. It's been six years. Six of the most haunted years of my life and I just want it to go away. When I hear her suck in a breath, I raise my eyes and meet her gaze.

"Wrist to elbow." She mimics my words. I grin a small but sad grin at her and shake my head.

"Your life isn't mine, darlin'. It isn't my place to take it." As the words leave my mouth, I know I've done worse things in the past. I've killed, I've taken lives that weren't mine, but she's different. Hers is different. She licks her lips as I watch her. Leaning forward, she stalls right in front of me. Her lips are a few inches from mine. I see the look in her eyes.

"You don't wanna lose it to me," I tell her watching the flicker of a blaze burn inside of her.

"What difference does it make if this is it for both of us?" she asks. I smell the alcohol on her breath. Something about the way she looks at me pulls at my insides.

"Are you really gonna do it? Don't you think there has to be somethin' else out there for you?" I ask her.

When the blaze slowly leaves her gaze, she pulls back a little and says, "I get it. I'm too fat."

The air thickens between us. The room seems to close in. She can't be serious, but the more I look at her, the more I can see she is. I lean closer, grabbing her around the back of her neck, pulling her face back to mine.

"You're perfect. There is nothin' about you that's fat or ugly. You are you." I touch my lips to hers softly and she sighs, opening up to me. I kiss her gently at first, wondering what the hell is wrong with me. Being gentle isn't in my nature,

11

yet for this girl, I'm doing it. Maybe it's the part of me that wants to help someone. Maybe it's the part that doesn't want to see her kill herself although I shouldn't give a damn seeing how I'm going to end my own life. I break our heated kiss long enough to pull my head back and look her in the eyes.

"I'm nobody to give it to," I tell her.

"You're somebody. You just don't see it in yourself," she says softly. Her words wrap around my heart and squeeze. I used to think I was somebody. I was until that night. "Please," she says so softly, I barely heard her.

I nod my head before I stand up. She watches me intently as I slide my cut down my arms before removing my shirt. Her eyes trail a line of fire over my chest before biting her lip. I grab a condom out of my back pocket before my boots are kicked to the side, jeans and boxers following. She watches me as I stroke myself, sliding the condom down my length.

"Can't do anything with your clothes on." I give her a sad smile. She hesitates. I climb onto the dirty floor on my knees in front of her. I reach for her shirt but she shakes her head no. I let her have that. It's her security and I won't take that away. I push her back onto her back and grab the front of her jeans, yanking them and her panties off with her shoes. She watches me but doesn't say a word as I climb between her thighs.

"Change your mind." I almost beg her. I don't want her first time to be like this. She deserves more than getting fucked on a dirty warehouse floor.

"No."

I slide a hand between her legs and watch as her eyes fall closed. Dragging my finger through her wetness, I'm surprised. She's this fucking wet for me? She doesn't know me. I hadn't touched her until just now. I grab my dick and tease her a little before pushing in. Her hands fly to my arms, gripping them. Her nails dig into my skin as I push through the barrier keeping us apart. I look down and watch the tears fall from her eyes.

"Look at me," I demand her. Her eyes open and those seas of blue lock on me. "It won't take away the pain." She nods her head slowly understanding what I mean.

I rock into her and moan at the feeling. I don't give a shit what anyone said to her. She's perfect. She's gorgeous. And for this moment, she's mine. I thrust a little harder as emotions run wild inside of me. That smile. Those eyes. The way they looked at me and pleaded with me to help when I was helpless myself. Sobs choke me as I fuck this poor girl roughly. All of it is too consuming. I'm drowning in my past and the feel of her beneath me. Her cries fall on deaf ears as the world around fades. When I finish and come inside of her, I pull out quickly and drop to the ground next to her. I can hear her sniffle but she doesn't move to get up.

"Are you still gonna do it?" I ask her knowing she knows what the question means.

"Are you?"

"Sleep on it, darlin'. You might feel different tomorrow, yeah?" The silence between us is almost eerie. We both lie here catching our breath but different things running around inside of us.

After what seems like forever she says, "Crow?"

"Yeah, darlin'?"

"Will you stay with me?"

Her words throw me off. I hadn't planned on living past midnight, but something deep inside of me says to do it, if only for her.

"Yeah, I will. Come here." I glance over but she doesn't move. "I wanna hold you," I tell her.

She turns her head and looks at me a second before scooting across the dirty floor. I reach my arm out and wrap it around her, pulling her head to my chest. I take a deep breath and sigh before I say, "Sleep now, beautiful. Tomorrow brings new light." She sighs and snuggles up against me. I lie there until I hear her breathing even out. Then I slowly fall asleep myself.

Chapter 3

I wake up to my back screaming in pain. When my head starts to pound I remember what I did last night. I glance down and the girl is already gone. I didn't even ask her name. Shaking my head, I think of what fucked up piece of shit I am. The funny thing is, she covered me with my own shirt. It's draped over my chest like a blanket. I should be thankful that she didn't decide to kill herself last night. I should be thankful that I didn't but I'm not.

Shoving myself up, I dress quickly as I take in the mess we made last night. Blood stains the dirty floor, but no one will ever know what it's from. This is one of the club's warehouses. We don't use it anymore. I'm probably the only one that ever sets foot in it. I stretch my back out as I walk out of the door and into the sunlight.

"Fuck," I mumble as I make my way to my bike. I dig through my saddle bag and pull out my cell, noticing I have a shit ton of missed calls and messages. I don't give a damn about those right now. I need a shower and a shave. I feel like I was hit by a goddamn bus and the smell of that girl still lingers on my skin. It's not a bad smell to have either. I shake my head knowing what I took from her last night. I shouldn't have done it, but in my drunken moment, I didn't want to see her hurting. It was overwhelming. If I could make her feel better even for a night, I wanted to fucking do it. I don't know where that part of me came from, but it felt good at the moment. Now I feel like a piece of shit for fucking her senseless and not asking her damn name. I'm sure she'll forget about me just the same as I will her. We will both go on with our daily shit lives and nothing about last night will even matter.

Grabbing my helmet, I throw it on before climbing on my bike. The guys knew what was happening last night. They knew I was off. I'm sure they are all wondering where the fuck I am or if I really killed myself this time. I rev up my bike and take off.

Thoughts consume my brain. I hate that I feel this way all the time, but even more, I hate that I was too much of a coward to take my own life last night. I set out to do just that when I saw her. Now I'm a little pissed that she got in the way of my plans. She fucking ruined what I was about to accomplish. The ride to the clubhouse doesn't take long, and as soon as I pull up to the gate, the prospect grins like a bitch. I flip him off and wave at him to open the gate before I pull in. I head straight toward my house too. Fuck the clubhouse.

Fuck the guys. I'm not in the mood to deal with any of it right now, but as soon as I take the second right and head to the end of the road, I see Smokey and Ruger sitting on my goddamn porch like watch dogs. I kill the engine and climb off as they watch me.

"Well, I'll be damned. I ain't never had a welcome home committee before," I say sarcastically as I walk up the front steps.

"Ain't never lost your shit for the whole night and not checked in either," Ruger growls as I sit in the seat next to him. He passes me a joint, which I gladly take.

"Yeah, well. Rough night," I tell him as I inhale.

Blowing out the ring of smoke, Smokey laughs. "I'll say. You smell like you had a few good rounds of pussy last night." He chuckles harder.

I shake my head and glance over at him and say, "I had a round alright. What are you bastards on my porch for?" Ruger leans back, putting his hands behind is head and sighs.

"Well, I need a bitch to ride out to Henley's with me. Someone who likes blood and guts. Figured you were my guy." He chuckles as I smile.

"Damn right I'm your guy. When we ridin'?" I ask, passing the joint to Smokey.

"As soon as you're ready. Hawk's pissed. Shipment was cancelled at the last minute. He wants to know why," Smokey tells me. I nod my head. Maybe I need to get bloody today. It would do me some good. No matter what the plan was last night, today is a new day and my brothers need me. I can play the part like any good actor. I can play the happy go lucky card and win a goddamn Emmy for it, but inside, I'm slowly dying. Just because it didn't happen last night doesn't mean I'm fixed.

"Let me grab a shower and I'm good." I shove out of the chair and head inside. As soon as I turn on the water, I hear my door close. I close my eyes as I step in wash away the reminder of last night.

"What?" I snap when I hear the footsteps come into the bathroom.

"Glad you came back, brother." Ruger's voice fills the room. I close my eyes as the warm water washes the blood from my body.

"It wasn't the right time," I tell him as I watch the red tinged water swirl at my feet.

"There's always a time, but you're right, Crow. This isn't yours, brother. You got more in you. Meet you outside."

I listen to him leave the room before I sigh. Maybe he's right. Maybe I have more in me, but if that's true, I'm not sure how. I've given about all I have to give. I'm still me though. I'm still Crow, the motherfucking Soulless Bastard.

Chapter 4

The ride out Henley's didn't take us very long. I like it out here. It's near the ocean and tourists. You might wonder why that's a good thing, but tourists are a good cover for us. They are always doing something stupid as fuck and we can make a lot of shit look like they caused it. Besides, when there are dead bodies and no one else around, it could have been a tourist.

"Look at this shit. No wonder the son of a bitch likes it here. No one can touch him without settin' off some kind of alarm to these people." Ruger flicks his cigarette to the ground as he looks around at all the people milling about over here. Henley wasn't stupid. He set up his clubhouse in an old retail store right in the heart of tourist country.

"Fuckin' bullshit. Looks like a pussy to me," I grumble as we walk toward the building.

"Bullshit? Or smart as fuck? He knows we'll be on at least fifteen store cameras, the bastard," Ruger chuckles. I follow along. He's right about that. There are so many shops around here, we are bound to be picked up on a few cameras.

"That's why we talk nicely and lead him out," Ruger says as he shrugs, pulling open the front door. The interior is not what you would expect. This may be an old retail business but it's set up like a clubhouse. There's a building inside a motherfucking building. Another door sits in front of us as Ruger and I share a glance. Walking up to the next door, I raise my hand and knock.

"I feel like I'm askin' some chick to the dance," I say with a laugh.

"You went to a dance?" Ruger asks, cocking his head to the side to look at me.

"Back in elementary school." This pulls a full blown laugh from Ruger just as the door opens.

"Who the fuck are you?" the guy thunders. Ruger and I share a glance before he steps up to the door.

"Look, motherfucker, that is no way to answer the goddamn door." Before I know what the fuck is happening, Ruger has the guy around the throat, walking him back into his own clubhouse. The man's eyes are wide and his face turns red.

"There's one way to get in," I mumble as I look around. In the matter of seconds, two more guys show up, guns in hand.

"Let him the fuck go," one of them growls. Ruger shoves the little prick away from him as we all watch him tumble to the floor and gasp for air.

"Why do you motherfuckers have to be so bitchy?" Ruger asks, wiping his hands down his jeans as if the man had dirtied them. I can't help but laugh. The man is off the hinges.

"We need to talk to Henley. Get him the fuck out here," I say as I wave my gun through the air.

"He ain't here," the smaller one says. Ruger takes a step toward him, me right behind him.

"Oh, he's here. I know he's here, and you know what else I know?" I say the closer we get. I can see they are just prospects guarding the fucking door. "I know that if you don't run your little ass back there and get him, my boy here will bend you both over. You know you've heard about Ruger, right?" I watch the look on their faces as Ruger grins at them. This fucker is truly out there.

"I'll be right back," one of them says.

I watch the other as he tries to remain stoic. Little shit. I want to punch the fuck out of him. I keep myself contained when I smell smoke. I see the swirls of smoke as they curl into the air, announcing Henley's arrival. He looks between the two of us but doesn't say anything. I don't like this fuck all that much. Never did. He is off. He's eerie as fuck. The motherfucker is smart as hell but has some kind of disability that causes him to speak slower than others. That doesn't make him any less lethal.

"You girls want somethin'?" he finally asks.

I chuckle when Ruger says, "You're goddamn right we do. We wanna know why that shipment was cancelled last minute."

Henley watches us. It's a little unnerving to have him staring you in the goddamn eye and know that his wheels are spinning to come up with an answer.

"We have a situation. I was plannin' on takin' a ride out to see you boys. Come on back," he says as he motions for us to follow.

I glance over at Ruger, but he just shrugs and follows behind Henley. I take that as my cue and do the same. The prospects step to the side allowing us to move freely. The back of the

24

clubhouse surprises me. It looks like a damn clubhouse. It amazes me to see this shit inside a retail area. Henley looks over his shoulder, taking a moment to form his words.

"You like it? You know no one bats a motherfuckin' eye at this place," he says. I nod my head as I keep glancing around me. There's a bar set up to the left. Stools of men line it drinking and having a good time. To the right there are some make shift rooms I can only assume they use to sleep in.

"Sit down. Rosie! Get 'em some beers," Henley roars. I sit in the chair and watch the girl I assume to be Rosie make her way to the bar before dragging my gaze to his.

"What's the problem, Henley? We need somethin' here," I tell him.

He pulls out a cigarette and lights it up before setting his lighter on his desk. The words are forming in that head of his. "Ancient Times MC. They seem to be movin' into the area. Tipped off a few cops as to the location of our stash. We're handlin' that but we had to relocate. Can't move shit until I handle them."

That's not what I wanted to hear, but I'm glad it wasn't some other bullshit like him trying to fuck us over. I blow out a breath and run my hand over my face.

"What are they after?" Ruger asks when Rosie hands us both a beer. She eyes Ruger wearily, but when her gaze comes to me, she winks.

I shake my head, irritated with myself. It isn't about her. It's about the girl from last night. How the hell do you fuck someone like that and not even ask her name? What kind of piece of shit does that make me? I know I use women like toilet paper, but fuck, that girl was different.

"Crow! Where the fuck you go, brother?" Ruger snaps at me. I shake my head, clearing all the thoughts of her and what I did to her.

"What?" I ask sounding a little more annoyed than I meant to.

"You think Hawk will go with the idea?" he asks me. I shrug not knowing what the fuck the idea even was.

"Goddamn, Crow. Get your head outta your fuckin' ass, brother," Ruger growls. I start to shove out of my chair when Ruger grabs my arm. "I know shit's off with you, Crow, but fuck." I nod my head and sit back in the chair. That was his way of apologizing. I take it at what it is.

Henley watches me for a long minute before he says, "Gettin' rid of ATs. You think Hawk will be down to help out with that?"

"Don't see why not. We've never had shit to do with them. What are they after?" I ask.

Henley shrugs, taking another long drag off his cigarette. "Not sure yet. Sent a few guys out on recon. I'll get with you once we know."

Ruger grunts taking his beer down in a few gulps. "Heard that. We'll let Hawk know what's goin' on. Next time ride out sooner. He was ready to shoot on sight," Ruger tells him. Henley nods his head as the words form.

"Heard that. I just had a lot of shit bein' handed down to me. Not just ATs. My old lady went into labor early. Kid's in the hospital. One of our guys got killed a week ago. Shit's been slammin' us." Damn. Hearing all that makes my problems look like nothing. I know in my mind they are horrible, but what Henley's facing is much worse.

"Fuck, brother. Sorry to hear all that," I tell him. Henley nods when I take down the rest of my beer. I set the bottle on the desk in front of me before shoving up.

"We'll get back with you soon," I tell him. Henley nods his head as Ruger and I head toward the door.

"Fuck. Who the hell knew shit was gettin' that real over here," Ruger says running his hand through his hair.

"Heard that. All he had to do was make a goddamn call though," I mumble as we head out the front door. As soon as we step outside, the hot California sun beats down on me.

"Fuck it's hot!"

Chapter 5

We ride around town for a while just checking shit out. Nothing seems out of the ordinary and at the moment there are no signs of the Ancients. I don't know if that's a good thing or not. I wanted to get my hands dirty today. I wanted to see something bleed but I guess I will have to settle for mentally torturing myself. I seem to be getting damn good at that. We make our way back toward home when I follow Ruger as he rolls to a stop in the parking lot of a small diner. I kill the engine and climb off, glaring over at him.

"Hungry?" I ask, teasing a little. Ruger grunts and sets his helmet on his seat.

"I ain't had no food since this mornin'. Big fucker like me needs nourishments," he says rubbing his stomach.

I chuckle as I follow him inside. The little chime over the door dingles announcing our entrance. All eyes seem to shift toward us but quickly go back to what they were doing. I shake my head, not in the mood to deal with the likes of the common assholes that run around this city.

"You gonna look pissed all day?" Ruger asks over his shoulder as I follow him to a booth by the window.

"Maybe. Who the fuck cares?" I ask as I slide in. As soon as we settle into our seats, the waitress walks over laying menus in front of us.

"What can I get you boys to drink?" she asks with the hint of flirtation in her voice. I don't look up because frankly, I don't give a shit.

"Beer and a water," I say, picking up my menu and eyeing my choices. Ruger orders his drinks as well, but I tune him out as he flirts with the girl.

"Hot piece of ass. I should get a piece but I wanna keep my nuts." He laughs. I shake my head and laugh along with him.

"How is shit with Kira?" I ask, setting my menu back down in front of me.

Ruger leans back in his seat and looks at me before he says, "Not bad. It's a little weird for me, brother. One chick? I mean, she don't mind bringin' in one of the whores to play but fuck. I don't want them touchin' my woman." He grunts again making me laugh.

"I feel you, brother. She's a good girl though. The guys seem to like her, like havin' her around," I add.

"What about you? You like her?" he asks. I shrug my shoulder and look at my hands.

"Doesn't matter what I think, but yeah. She's good to you. It's about time you had one like that. You ever need a third player, call me in," I joke.

Ruger laughs before he says, "Fuck that. You ain't touchin' her either."

The waitress sets our drinks on the table before we both order chicken wings. It doesn't take long before we are both filled the fuck up with food. I lean back in my seat, fully sated. I grab my beer and take another pull when I hear commotion behind me. I don't turn to look but Ruger leans to the left and takes a look. He shakes his head when his eyes come back to meet mine.

"What is it with men and a women's weight? I never understood that shit. So the fuck what if she's bigger?"

I raise an eyebrow at him. I've never heard that leave his mouth before. That's a new side of Ruger I didn't see.

"Since when don't you give a shit?" I ask needing to know what the hell is with him.

"Since I don't give a shit. A woman is a woman. Don't matter her size. It matters what she can do for you," he chuckles.

The longer I sit here, the more I can hear what's being said behind me. I glare at Ruger as heat rises inside of me. I feel it crawling up my neck and I know my disgust is playing on my face. I may be a woman user but I sure as hell don't tolerate that shit that's happening behind me.

"Don't do it," Ruger says as a shit eating grin crosses his face knowing damn good and well I'm going to do it.

I swallow hard, trying to focus on anything but these little pansy fucks behind me. When I hear the words "You are so disgusting" leave the fuckers lips, I slide out of the booth. Ruger laughs as I spin around and face the son of a bitch.

"Hey!" I roar pulling his attention. I don't even look at the woman he's talking to. It doesn't matter to me what she looks like.

"Who the hell are you talking to?" the punk asks looking me up and down.

"Didn't your momma teach you how to talk to women?" I growl as my hands clench at my side. Someone makes a noise next to me. I assume it's one of the girls but I don't stop myself to check. My focus is on this punk.

"Fuck you, man. You look at her?" he asks me. I slowly drag my gaze over to the girl and gasp. It's her.

"You," I say in disbelief.

She looks up and her big blue eyes find mine. "Crow," she says. Shock is laced in her words and her body is stiff, completely unsure of what to do.

My heart leaps in my chest a little. I didn't expect to see her again, but I find that it's a good surprise. She gives me a small smile before I look back at the bastard in question.

"Apologize," I growl as the asshole stands there with a smirk on his face. I want nothing more than to rip his little lip ring out and shove it down his throat. The punk laughs when I reach up and grab him by the throat.

"I said apologize to her." I jerk his face around as he looks at her.

"Figures you'd know the pig," he mumbles before I squeeze harder.

"Know her? Kid, I fucked her. She has one hell of a pussy between those sexy thighs, now fuckin' apologize before I snap your goddamn neck," I growl.

"Wait, what? Lyric? What the hell?" her friend across from her says.

I look at the girl. Lyric. Fuck that's a hot ass name too. Lyric's cheeks turn pink, making me grin just a little.

"Oh shit. He done fucked that girl," Ruger chuckles behind me. I don't turn to look at the asshole either.

"I'm givin' you one more second to stay silent. Then I'm fuckin' your world up," I tell the prick that gasps for air.

"Sorry," he says before I shove him back. I watch him stumble and fall to his ass before he scoots away from me.

"Punk ass," I mumble dragging my gaze back to hers.

"You're still alive," she says with a smile on her face. Fuck, look at her. She's so damn beautiful.

"Yeah, but I'm barely breathin'. Glad to see you still walkin' though. Finish your meal. He won't fuck you with anymore," I tell her as I turn to Ruger. He stands next to the table with a shit eating grin on his face. One I'd like to slap it the fuck off. I hate that he knows exactly what I did with her now. Not that it matters.

"You ready?" I ask walking past him, reaching into my pocket and tossing some cash on the table.

"Oh, I'm ready. Ready to hear all about that pussy you got," he says as he follows me out the door. I head toward my bike when I hear her.

"Crow!"

Chapter 6

I look over my shoulder and see her standing there. I'm not sure what the look is in her eyes. She looks to be torn between what she wants to say to me and walking away from it all. If it was any other day I would want her to walk, but something about her tugs at my heart. Something deep inside of me yearns to feel her lips once more. It's a fucked up feeling to have but it's there all the same. And I'm not going to fight it.

"You have a minute?" she asks, chewing on her bottom lip. Fuck. I glance over at Ruger.

He lifts his chin and says, "I'll meet you at home, brother. We don't have shit to do tonight."

I nod once and turn back to Lyric. Her big blue eyes looking anywhere but at me. I wonder if she's nervous? I wonder what she even wants. I close the distance between us, standing a few inches from her. I can smell her perfume. Flowers and candy. That's what she fucking smells like.

"Didn't think I'd see you again," I say softly. She still doesn't look at me and for some reason that pisses me off. I reach up and pull her chin into my hand forcing her gaze to move with it. "You look good," I tell her. Her cheeks flush again and I can't help but smile.

"I just wanted to say thank you. Not just for what you did in there but that night. I thought about waking you up. You looked so at peace and I didn't want to bother you," she says sweetly. My chest tightens as the memory of that night comes rushing back.

"You covered me up," I say. She furrows her brows, a little crease forming between her eyes.

"So?" she asks, not really understanding what I mean.

"You took the time to think about me in the moment. It was nice," I tell her. No one has ever been that nice to me. Not when I was a kid. Not as an adult. Never.

"It's common curtesy." She smiles as I let my hand fall to my side. I shake my head just as her friend comes storming out.

"I want to know who you are and when you fucked my friend. In fact, I want to know why I wasn't informed that you were out fucking some hot piece of man!" the little red head says as she glances from me to her friend. She's a spunky little thing. "Which one of you are going to answer me?" she asks with her hands on her hips.

"You're a little spitfire. I like it," I say as I look down at the woman who can't be more than five feet tall. Lyric takes a step back, something dark crossing her features. She stands off to the side while her friend questions me. What the hell is wrong with her? Why did she move away? I don't answer one word that red is throwing at me. I walk over to Lyric and rest my hand on her hip.

"Talk to me. What's goin' on in that pretty head of yours?" I drown out the words that her friend is still spouting off behind us. All I see is her.

"She's prettier. She would be better for you to talk to."

Fuck! With my free hand, I reach up and grab her around the back of her neck, pulling her face to meet mine. I run my tongue over the seam of her lips, hearing a gasp escape her. As soon as her mouth opens, I move in. I let my tongue explore hers. I let her moans fall into my mouth. I kiss her like a woman should be kissed. When I pull back, we're both breathless. I rest my forehead against hers, looking into those deep blue eyes.

"I don't wanna talk to her. In fact, she isn't my type," I say before I press my lips to hers once more.

"Oh no you didn't! That is my best friend. If you hurt her I will shove my foot up your ass!" the girl roars behind me. Lyric and I both laugh against each other's lips before she moves around me.

"He can't hurt me. We aren't together, Sherry," Lyric says as she stands next to her friend. I turn slowly to face the two of them, crossing my arms over my chest. Sherry's mouth hangs open as she looks at my arms bulging. I want to laugh but Lyric just rolls her eyes.

"We met under some uncomfortable circumstances. Neither of us were in our right minds and we kinda used that on each other," I inform the girl. Lyric smiles proudly as if sleeping with me was the best part of her life.

"Used it on each other? I'd say you did more than that. She hasn't smiled this much in…well ever." Sherry says, looking up at her friend. I can see the love there. It's not all the different from me and the guys.

"Glad I could help then," I say as I start to walk past them again. Something inside of me clenches. Thoughts swirl around my head. I find myself turning back to find them both watching me.

"You wanna go for a ride?" I ask Lyric. Her smile gets bigger and brighter. She nods her head before hugging her friend.

"Take care of her!" Sherry yells at me. I nod and give her a two finger salute all the while watching Lyric walk toward me.

"You ever been on one?" I nod toward my bike. Lyric's eyebrows shoot up, her arms crossing over her chest.

"I'm pretty sure if my big ass gets on there, the tire will go flat," she says. She doesn't sound as if the words she just said even bother her; it's like she's accepted it as fact. It does me though. I shake my head and pinch the bridge of my nose. I want to say something but I don't know her well enough to do that.

"Not a chance. Come on," I tell her. She walks slowly toward me as I hold the helmet up to her. She takes in her hands and slides it on her head, her long hair hanging out of the sides. Damn, she looks good like that.

"What are you staring at?" she finally asks after God only knows how long I've stared at her.

"You look fuckin' gorgeous. Come on." I hold my hand out to her to help her get on the bike. She throws her leg over and thoughts of what lies between them resurface in my mind. I shake my head to rid the thoughts, climbing on in front of her.

"Hold on tight, baby," I tell her as I reach back and pull her hands around my waist. The feel of her warmth consumes me. I like feeling her there. I don't know her for shit, but I like how I feel when she's this close to me. I may be fucking insane, but for the moment, I'm running with it. I rev up my bike when I hear Lyric squeal behind me. I glance over my shoulder at the smile on her face, giving her one back before pulling out of the parking lot and onto the open road. I know I just came back from near the beach, but I want to go back. I like it there. I feel a sense of calmness when I'm there.

We ride through town until I find a place to park. I climb off first, offering her my hand to help her off. After I take of her helmet and run my fingers through her windblown hair, I grab her hand in mine.

"Lyric, huh? Unique name," I say her as I walk us toward the pier. The sand shifts under my boots but everything in the world is calm in this moment.

"My mom was a singer. She always loved it. She wanted me to be just like her so she named me Lyric," she explains, a smile on her face.

"It's a good name. You sing?" I ask her.

Her smile slowly fades before she says, "Not in public anymore. I used to. I was in plays and all kinds of things when I was younger. After mom died, it didn't seem important anymore." The sadness creeps across her face. It's like a punch to the gut.

"Your dad?" I ask. Lyric shakes her head.

"No dad. He left when mom was pregnant. She married Luther when I was little. He was okay at first, I guess. After mom died, he changed. He used me to take out his anger," she says as we walk up the ramp of the pier.

"Had to be hard for you. That part of the cuttin'?" I ask.

Lyric doesn't answer, just squeezes my hand a little tighter as we walk down the dark pier. When we hit the end, I motion for her to sit on the bench. Lyric sits as I sit next to her waiting to hear what else she has to say. She seems to take a moment to get her thoughts together.

"It gave me a good feeling. It's hard to explain. I feel alive when I cut myself. I can see the blood on my skin and I know I'm alive," she says, looking over at me. Her hair blows in the wind as her eyes stay on mine. I reach up and brush it away from her face.

"Pain is a mask. We all wear it at times. Some of us don't take it off. When all you have left is the pain, it will eat you alive. You can't let it do that," I tell her before leaning in and pressing my lips to hers. She tastes so damn perfect on my tongue. So perfect that I know I want more.

Chapter 7

Lyric has been around for over a month now, almost nonstop. She keeps me sane at times. Something about her being close to me settles something deep inside of me. Maybe it's because we both hurt. Maybe we have a connection that no one else has. Who the fuck knows - I just know that I like when she's near. Like right now, lying in bed and touching her – it soothes something in me.

I haven't taken her to the clubhouse, and I haven't let any of the guys aside from Ruger meet her. This isn't a boyfriend-girlfriend type relationship. This is me and her. Two broken and lost souls trying to ease the other's pain for a little while.

"So, there will be drinking?" she asks as she runs her fingers over my chest. Damn it feels so good having her touch me. I play in her hair as her as she continues her travels over my skin.

"Sweetheart, of course, there will be drinkin'. It's what we do," I tease her.

"I don't know, Crow. I get a little…loose when I drink," she says with a giggle. I roll her onto her back and loom over her raising my eyebrow.

"Loose? As in?" I say teasing her slightly. Lyric giggles and shoves at me but I just lean in and kiss her soft lips.

"Loose as in I can't control my actions and I typically belt out songs," she says raising her head so that her lips meet mine. I thread my fingers in her hair and kiss her roughly. I grind against her, my free hand roaming down her side and up under her shirt.

"One day, this thing is comin' off," I warn her as I toy with her nipples. Lyric moans and makes my dick harder. "I get why you want it on, but I want to see all of you Lyric." I lick her bottom lip before pulling it between my teeth.

"I know. Just not yet, okay?" she says. I smile at her and check the time before climbing off the bed. Reaching into the dresser, I pull out a t-shirt and toss it to her. She holds it in her hand as if I've lost my mind or the shirt might attack her. Either way, it's ridiculous.

"What?" I ask, confused.

"What is this?" She sits up and looks down at the shirt in her hands.

"That," I say pointing at it, "is my shirt. Put it on. You slept in yours," I remind her. Her eyes jerk to mine, something's off in them.

"What now? You don't like my shirt?" I ask playing with her. I hold my hand over my heart to fake emotion.

Lyric shakes her head before looking away. "I get that guys think it's sexy for the woman to wear his shirt, but that's when it looks like a dress on her. This won't fit me." I sigh and run my hand through my hair.

"It will fit you and you will look sexy as fuck in it. You have to stop downin' yourself like that, Lyric," I tell her. My patience with this "I'm fat thing" is wearing thin. I've had about all I care to hear about it.

"I'm not, Crow. I'm telling the damn truth. I'm too fat to wear your clothes," she snaps.

"What size is that goddamn shirt you have on?" I snap back.

"An extra extra large," she says almost sounding embarrassed.

"Well, what the fuck do you know? So is mine! Put it on or I will do it for you, Lyric," I demand. She looks up at me with tears in those blue eyes. I walk over and sit on the edge of the bed, grabbing her face in my hand.

"I get why you feel like you do. I don't see you like that. I think that you look sexy as hell in whatever the fuck you have on. Don't compare yourself to others. You aren't them." I press a kiss to her forehead before standing and watching her.

"You're really going to make me wear your shirt?" she asks as if she hasn't learned who the boss is by now.

"Yeah. When we are done at the party, I am gonna have fun peelin' you out of that shirt. You're gonna give me all of you, Lyric," I tell her before turning and heading into the bathroom. I can hear her little huff and it makes me smile. I understand her reasoning. I get why she wants to be covered up, but I also know that I want to see all of her. I want to kiss every inch of her body. I want to feel her skin pressed against me in every way possible. I wash my face quickly and pull my boxers and jeans on before heading back into the room. I step short when I see her. She stands there with her boy short lacey underwear in plain view. My shirt hangs to her hips. Fuck, her long legs are a sight to see. My dick jerks liking what he sees too.

"You look fuckin' sexy as hell," I say, my voice raspy. She does this shit to me. She makes me feel like the world is worth living in. Lyric slowly turns to face me, a smile playing at her lips.

"It doesn't fit me like a dress," she says, tugging at the hem of the shirt. I take long strides, stopping in front of her.

"Fuck a dress. I can see those sexy thighs anytime I want like this. No clothes to remove. Shit, Lyric. I'm hard again," I say as I grab her hand and bring it to my dick. She wraps her fingers around it, squeezing slightly but enough to make me groan.

"Fuck. We ain't never gonna get to the party," I say, pushing her back against the bed. I climb between her legs, grinding my painfully hard dick against her. Her panties are already soaked, I saw that the moment I laid her down. I like that she wants me like that. I like that I can turn her on without even touching her.

"I'm gonna take you hard and fast. I'm so fuckin' horny right now, Lyric," I tell her as I reach down and unbutton my jeans. I pull my dick free, rubbing against her. Her body shudders with every touch of me. Lyric's hand slides down between us, yanking at her panties.

"I see someone is as horny as me?" I tease her. I shove off her and stand at the edge of the bed, watching her pull her panties off quickly and toss them to the side. When she looks up at me, her blue eyes call to me. They beg me, and God fucking help, me I fall into them. I climb back on the bed, nudging her legs apart. I reach over to the nightstand, grabbing a condom. I rip it open and roll it on in record time before sliding inside of her. This has become one of my favorite places to be. Buried inside Lyric takes everything else away. The pain. The hate. The anger. It all fades when I'm inside of her.

I lift her leg up and hike it up on my hip as I thrust into her like a mad man. Her cries are music to my ears. Her moans wrap around my throat and cut off all oxygen. She suffocates me with her lips. I want all of this woman and I can't for the life of me understand why. I don't want to live. I still want to die. I can feel it in the pit of my stomach but something with Lyric makes me hold on to another day. It makes me dream of a life that I can never have. Those thoughts are what choke me.

I slam into her as I take out my frustration. The knowing that I can't ever have a life that I wanted. The knowing that at some point I'm going to have to leave Lyric alone. The thought kills me inside but I thrust harder, enjoying the way her pussy clamps around me, holding me close to her. This is all I need right now. She is all I need. She's like air and my lungs burn to have her. It's wrong. It's very wrong because when this is over, when my life is over, it will crush her. I've let her become a drug that masks the pain, but when it's all over with she will be the one left hurting. But I'm too selfish to let her go.

"Come with me, Lyric!" I growl as I change my angle. Lyric grips my arms roughly as I feel her body begin to tremble. I thrust and grunt releasing inside of her as she falls apart beneath me. I lower my head take her lips with mine as her breathing comes out heavily. I rest my head against hers and sigh.

"After this party, that shirt comes off. I want those nipples in my hands and mouth. Got me?" I look her in the eyes, and I think that at this moment she would give me anything I asked for. She's completely sated as she nods her head slowly. I grin and kiss her again.

Chapter 8

Holding Lyric's hand in mine feels right. The world slows down when she's touching me. She's my angel. That's one thing I've learned about her. No matter what haunts her deep inside, she's an angel. I want her to shine brightly with her halo. I want her to spread her wings and fly, but she needs that extra push. Of all the wrong doings in my life, I want Lyric to be the right thing. I want to be the one who can show her just how perfect she is. How much she truly has inside of her. I don't care what it takes to do it. I don't care how many bridges I have to burn down to get her there, that's what I want for her. I've never turned my back on things that I've wanted in the past and I sure as hell won't do it now.

"What if they all hate me?" she asks nervously as we walk closer to the clubhouse. The music is pounding through the speakers, echoing through the night.

"Who gives a fuck? I told you, all that matters is me." I nudge her with my elbow. Lyric giggles and my heart beats faster. I love hearing her sound happy. I know there are days when she tries to hide her pain from me. I can see it and I let her have some space, but at the end of the day, I want to take it all away from her. I don't want her to feel that way. All I want is to see her smile.

"I mean it, Crow. I'm sure I don't look like the rest of the girls," she mumbles.

I take a deep breath and blow it out before releasing her hand. I move to stand in front of her, my hands resting on my hips. Lyric watches me; she has to know what's coming. We do this shit all the time, and frankly, I'm sick of hearing her put herself down all the time.

"Do I look like the kind of guy who gives a fuck?" I ask her seriously. Lyric looks at me while she chews her bottom lip.

"No."

"No. You're goddamn right. I don't give a fuck what people think, and do you know why?" I ask her. She looks away and that pisses me off. I reach up and grab her face in my hand forcing her to look at me. "Do you?" I ask again. Lyric shakes her head before I say, "Because no one matters but you. What you think of yourself is what's important. What they think? Fuck what they think, Lyric. They don't know you inside. They don't know your hopes and dreams. They don't know what you could be. You do. You have to stop. I can't handle listenin' to you down yourself all the time. I thought I was doin' a pretty good job showin' you what I see, but I guess I'm failin'." I drop her face from my hands and turn on my heel, walking toward the clubhouse. I didn't miss the sob that escaped her. I can't help her if she doesn't listen. I can't help her if she doesn't see what I see.

Before I can blink an eye, Lyric walks past me and pulls the clubhouse door open. She doesn't look back at me. She holds her head high. I watch her take a deep breath before finally glancing over her shoulder and giving me a wink and a smile. I shake my head and smile back. As soon as she walks through the door, I'm behind her. My hands wrap around her waist, pulling her back into me.

"Sexy. Confident. Fearless. That's what I see, Lyric," I whisper in her ear. We get a few stares but I don't pay attention. I know the bitches around here are used to us dragging home some bone thin women, but Lyric is something else. She's more than just a body type. I press a kiss behind her ear before I move to stand next to her. Intertwining our fingers, I pull her along toward the bar. She doesn't hesitate and that again makes me smile.

"Where the fuck you been?" Smokey asks, eyeing Lyric up and down before dragging his eyes to meet mine. I grin that cocky ass grin at him.

"Gettin' my dick wet," I chuckle. Lyric gasps but only smiles over at me.

"This is Smokey. Our VP. This is my girl Lyric." I introduce them. The other guys are pretty hardcore when it comes to their women. They are ruthless and can be mean. I think I stand out in that sense; I'm not like that. I don't want to hurt my woman. Never have.

"Good to meet you. About time you let this motherfucker out of the bed. He has work to do," Smokey says in a playful tone, but I get the underlying hint. I know I've been pretty far out of shit over the last month but I feel like it was needed.

"Yeah, yeah. I can't help it if she has the best pussy around." I fuck with him right back. I catch Lyric out of the corner of my eye with a blush creeping up her cheeks.

"Hey, Bray! Come here a minute," I holler when I see her. Bray walks over with a smile before she stops and leans against the bar.

"How you been, Crow? Haven't seen you much lately," she says sweetly.

I like Bray. We all do. She calms that beast inside of Smokey, although those two have a sick relationship.

"This is my girl Lyric. You think you can introduce her to some of the girls for me? Need to talk to your man," I tell her. Bray lights up as she pulls Lyric into an awkward hug. Lyric goes with it so I don't say anything.

"Of course, I will. Come on," Bray says excitedly as she grips Lyric's hand. Lyric's eyes dart to mine before I lean in and press a kiss to her lips.

"You're fine. You got this. I believe in you, baby. You can handle this just fine," I tell her. Her smile fades. Her eyes fill with tears before I kiss her once more.

"Don't do that, Lyric. You've come too far to turn back now, sweetheart. Be who I know you can be." One more kiss and Bray drags her off. I watch her go before Smokey throws an arm around my neck.

"What's with this one?" he asks. I glance over at him before pulling my gaze back to her and shrug.

"She makes feel safe. Like nothin' else matters," I tell him.

"That's a good thing. You haven't had that in years, brother," he reminds me as if I didn't know.

"Don't get excited, Smokey. It changes nothin'. If anything, I'm doin' this for her," I inform him. His arm tenses around me before I look back over at him.

"See how it goes, brother. Maybe in time it will heal you both. I like her. I see the difference in you," Smokey says. I huff out a breath and pull out of his grasp.

"Doesn't mean shit, Smokey! End game is still the same brother, I've just taken the long way around." I nod over at Lyric before grabbing a beer. Smokey doesn't look happy with what I said but that's life, isn't it? You live and you learn. You lose and die. I'm on the losing end no matter how much I wish it wasn't true. The guys don't understand this part of me. They don't understand what I feel and what haunts me. If only they could see those eyes that I see every night in my dreams, they would understand then. They would feel what I do and they would hate it. It would eat them alive the way it does me.

I reach up and run my hand through my hair, letting my fingers travel over the scar. The reminder of how useless I was. The reminder of what was taken from me and what I can never get back. This goddamn scar!

Chapter 9

The more I drink, the easier it is to breath. I'm not sure how much I've drank, but I know my body is numb. The pain is suffocated for the moment. The thoughts are hiding in the sea of alcohol that swim around inside of me. I zone out until I hear the music change. A song I've never fucking heard of comes over the speakers, but that's not what pulls my attention. It's Lyric. That beautiful creature standing near the DJ booth with the mic in her hand. Her eyes dance around the room when she opens her mouth and sings. People stop what they're doing to look at her. Hell, I look at her.

"How can you see into my eyes like open doors?

Leading you down, into my core

Where I've become so numb, without a soul

My spirit's sleeping somewhere cold

Until you find it there, and lead it back home..."

The words keep flowing out of her and my heart starts beating faster. She said she could sing, but this is something more. She's putting her heart out there on the line in front of a bunch of fucking strangers. People she doesn't know and shouldn't trust. Ruthless killers surround her and there she is, the angel amongst the devils. I shake my head, grabbing another beer before making my way closer to her. I stand off to the side, my hip leaning into the wall as I take her in. That right there is the real Lyric. That's the girl who hides under what this world has made her. She's got talent. She has a purpose in life. Chills race up my spine as she sings her heart out. I can't help but smile.

When the song's over, the room explodes. Everyone is screaming and whistling for her. The girls all rush her with the exception of a few club whores who are too worried about getting a dick in their mouth. She doesn't notice any of them. Her eyes are locked on me. She moves through the crowd thanking them but those seas of blue stay on me, holding me hostage. The closer she gets, the more I know I'm on the losing end of this battle. The way I feel when I'm with her. The way she looks at me. All of it. I'm losing.

"I told you not to let me drink so much!" She giggles as I wrap my hands around her waist, and drag her against me.

"That was beautiful. I've never heard anything like that, baby. You're an angel," I tell her before pressing my lips to hers. I kiss her hard. I force my tongue into her mouth before she can stop me. I spin her around, so her back is pinned to the wall as I grind against her. She tastes like my own slice of heaven. She feels so fucking soft against me. I kiss her jaw and down her neck, feeling her body tremble when Hawk ruins it all.

"Church now! We have a situation."

I groan when I hear it. I don't want to break this moment. I don't want to stop what I've started. Reluctantly I pull away from her. Her lips are swollen from my kiss. Her eyes are glossy with lust. Fuck!

"I gotta go in there for a while. Not sure how long it will take. You can wait here or at the house," I tell her breathlessly as I look at her lips. Lyric smiles, pulling my eyes to hers.

"I'll wait."

"Good." I press one last kiss before pulling away from her. I walk toward the other side of the room ready for church when I call out over my shoulder, "Stay away from the bar. I want you to sober up before I fuck you!" Lyric laughs out loud, her eyes catching on mine.

"I said I'd wait, I didn't say where," she teases.

Fuck, I'm falling to far into this girl. I shake my head and smile as I walk into the meeting room.

"What the fuck you so happy about?" Hawk asks as soon as I step foot in the door.

"Not a goddamn thing."

"He's got some new pussy," Ruger hollers from the other side of the table and laughs.

"That your piece of ass out there? The big one?" Hawk cocks his head to the side and looks at me. He's pushing his luck with me.

"The big one? Since when does pussy come in sizes?" I ask with a growl. The room is becoming heated. I can feel that warmth as it spreads through me, readying me for a war if that's what needs to be. The guys all know I'm not like them in the women department. I may let it slide because they are my brothers, but when it comes to mine? Not a chance in hell.

"Since Julia has one the size of Texas!" Draven announces breaking the tension. Hawk laughs but his eyes stay on me. He knows I won't hesitate to throw a blow, not even at my own president.

"Sit down you bunch of bastards. Henley called. Seems they have a little Ancient situation. They have one of their soldiers at their clubhouse. From what they can gather, this little fuck killed one of their women. Not sure who or what the fuck for, but that means a war for them. We ain't involved at this point aside from Henley wantin' us to take over the prisoner. We have dungeon where they don't. A few of you have seen their set up. They can't keep him hidden that long. Basically that puts us right in the middle of their motherfuckin' war. The question is, do we want in? Ancients ain't shit to us but Henley is. We don't back them, we lose that alliance. We do back them, we're in a war just the same as they are. Bastards have never had an issue with Henley's boys before and I don't see one now. This goes to vote though. If we do this, we need to move that asshole out here tonight. We need to let him settle down there for a while and see what it is that's happenin' amongst the Ancient. We'll need recon. You guys know the fuckin' drill, I don't need to repeat that shit. We vote it. Now," Hawk growls as I glance around at the guys. I'm all for getting bloody. Hell, I've known Henley for damn near as long as I've been alive. He's always been good to us.

"I'm in," I say before Hawk looks to the rest of the guys. I hear a few no's come in but majority always rules.

"We do this. Crow, Ruger, and Draven - you three ride out there and get the little fuck. Get Micky to set up the dungeon for our visitor. While you're out there, see what you can get on the fuckin' Ancients. I want to know what the hell we're dealin' with. Not just this pansy fuck. All of it!" Hawk looks around the table before slamming the gavel down. We all shove out of our seats and head toward the door. Hawk clears his throat, pulling my attention.

"You got your head right?" he asks me.

What the fuck is this shit?

"Fuck yeah, I do. When do I not?" I ask with a growl. It vibrates through my body. I can feel myself getting edgier by the second. Why the fuck is he after my ass all of a sudden?

"I know what you went out to do, Crow. I know every goddamn year you go out there, but this time you brought somethin' back." I shake my head confused by what he's saying. "That girl. She makes you smile. Is that permanent?" he asks, his head cocked to the side. I want to slam my fist into his mouth. I want to fuck him up for even asking about her.

"No," I say as I turn on my heel and leave the room. She isn't permanent. Yeah, I like her. I like having her around, but that doesn't change what's set in my soul. That doesn't pull the darkness out of me or take away the nightmares. It doesn't change what happened to me before and it sure as hell doesn't change what I plan on doing.

Chapter 10

I pace the area outside the back of Henley's clubhouse with a cigarette hanging from my lips. Lyric was gone when I came out from the meeting. She was drunk but the prospect said he called her a cab. I didn't know if I wanted to break his fucking neck or thank him for doing it. I wanted her there when I got back. Nothing I can do now though. It isn't like she lived with me although she's always around. I texted her a million times to make sure she got home safely but she hasn't answered me. Part of me wants to say fuck this job and go see her. The other part knows I need to let her have her space. As much as I like having her around, she might not like it as much as I do.

My head throbs from the alcohol I consumed earlier. My insides roll. I take a long drag before looking around. I can smell the ocean from here. It's that fucking close. The salty air surrounds me a I lean against the brick wall of the building. So many thoughts eat away at me. Why couldn't I have been different? Why couldn't I have been a better person? Nothing I can do now will fix the past. Nothing I can say will change what happened all those years ago. Some people say time can heal. They lie. Time does nothing but taunt you with another year that you don't have what you so desperately want. Time doesn't heal, it kills. It kills tiny pieces of you. It kills me every fucking day. And the worst part? When I close my eyes at night, I can feel myself drifting a little further away each time. I know my end is coming. It's only a matter of time. The grim reaper will only let you live on borrowed time for so long before he wants it back. I've been on the threshold before. I've been on the edge of hell and I nearly fell into the fire. I wish more times than not that I did fall. I wish this life was over and everything that it holds against me could be done. The back door opens, interrupting my thoughts and clearing my head immediately, and Draven walks out looking happy.

"We clear back here?" he asks. I nod my head and go to open the back of the van. I look around once more before he motions for the guys to bring him out. Slung into between Smokey and Ruger, the guy hangs limply. I chuckle a little when I see the blade in his leg.

"Didn't wanna walk?" I motion toward it making Ruger laugh.

"You know me, brother. I gave him the option. He chose wrong," he says nonchalantly as they toss him into the back of the van like a piece of trash. The sight sends memories rushing me. I feel dizzy when Ruger's at my side, holding me up.

"Shit. You ok? What the fuck?" he asks, clearly concerned. I shake my head, my cigarette falling to the ground at our feet.

"I'm fine. You need me?" I ask, pulling my shit together. I look up at Ruger, he just shakes his head.

"You ridin' alone?" he asks me. I nod once and I can see his jaw clench.

"I'll be fine, brother. I just need a few." Ruger watches me intently while the others finish up with Henley. I don't listen in, and frankly, I don't care. I need some air. I need to breath. I feel like I'm suffocating inside myself.

"Fine. You ain't back tomorrow, I'm comin' to look for you," he says as he points at me.

I nod my head and turn on my heel walking toward my bike. The whole situation is becoming more than I can handle. I don't know why the memories keep coming back to me. It's like photographs, pictures that keep flashing through my head. For years and years they've played on repeat to the point I feel like my sanity is slipping away.

Throwing my leg over my bike, I pull my helmet on my head. I can't focus. I can't see the light anymore. I'm drowning in all that is darkness and all that is hell. It's eating me alive and I can almost literally feel it.

I rev up my bike and haul ass away from the clubhouse. I don't know where I'm going and I don't care. I just need the space and I need the open road to try and take away some of the visions that are suffocating me. That face. Those eyes. The way they pleaded with me and there was nothing I could do. I don't know why I survived that. I don't know why I was taken too. That thought alone pisses me off further. It should have been me! It was always destined to be me but somehow the universe decided to fuck me. It plotted against me and ruined my goddamn life at the same time it stole my breath away. I hate the world. I hate everything in it!

I speed up hoping the wind whipping around me will somehow blow all the memories back in place. Back in the recesses of my mind where they belong, where I so desperately need them to be. The closer they get, the more I can feel them. It kills me. It's ripping my heart in half. That ache is something I never want anyone else to feel. The pain that etches its way inside of my heart and holds tightly.

I scream at the top of my lungs, until my chest hurts as I increase my speed. The phantoms, the ghosts, the parts that I kept locked away are slowly seeping into me. There is nothing I can do, so give up and let the pain take over me. I close my eyes. I let it all settle in my chest and then, only then do I hear a little voice say, "It's not your time." I pop my eyes open expecting to see someone but all I see the curve ahead that I'm about to miss. I try to right my bike as it all happens in slow motion. Maybe this is it. Maybe this will kill me. It will take away all the pain. The rage, the hate. It all has to disappear right now.

The bike shifts as I loosen my grip on the handlebars, willing death to come and wrap its icy cold fingers around my heart and drag me to the pits of hell. I close my eyes as I feel all control slowly slipping away as the beast between my legs shifts and swivels out of control. The last thing I remember is my helmet smashing against the pavement before the fires of hell slowly sweep over me.

Chapter 11

"Go fuck yourself, you skinny little prick. Don't you have some kind of fruit to go vomit up before you get too fat?" Her voice sends chills down my spine. It's not just her voice though, it's the words that are leaving her mouth. I can't believe she actually said them. I try to chuckle and it hurts like hell.

"Shit. You're awake?" Her voice calms and I feel her hand wrap around mine.

"Should I ask what that was about?" I say, my voice sounding strangled and rocky.

"Not right now. Are you in pain?" she asks sounding a little helpless.

"Not really," I lie as I pry my eyes open. Lyric stands over me, her long hair hanging like a curtain around her face. Her big blue eyes, puffy and red. She looks tired. I blink harder when I notice the bruise that's around her eye. I squint my eyes and blink a few more times trying to be clear on what I'm seeing right now.

"What the fuck happened to you?" The growl that rips through me sends pain shooting through my chest. I cough and try to catch my breath but the pain is almost unbearable.

69

"Stop, Crow. You need to calm down. I'm fine. Let's worry about you," she says, her hand resting on my shoulder. Her warmth is something I missed.

"You left," I say softly, as I lay my head back, closing my eyes.

"I needed some time. This is all going so quickly. You, the clubhouse, the girls. My life. It's spinning out of control. I'm sorry," she says, and that's when I feel it. A tear drops onto my cheek. I open my eyes and see her crying over me with her eyes closed. I raise my hand to her cheek, her eyes instantly opening.

"If you need time away from me, take it. You come first, Lyric. Always remember that," I tell her. She brings her hand up to cover mine and once again the world slows down. Nothing else matters but her.

Lyric shakes her head and says, "No. I just needed to breathe. You're the best thing that has happened to me, Crow."

If only she knew I felt the same way about her. But I can't tell her. I want to but there is no way. I won't leave her in this world when the time comes knowing that. She will fall apart and that's not what I want for her. I shift my hand and bring our fingers together, bringing them to my lips. I press a small kiss on her hand before I look back up at her.

"Not today but you will tell me." I nod toward her eye. She gives me a small smile before she nods.

"The guys are out there. I should probably go so they can come in," she says softly. I squeeze her hand tighter, not wanting her to go anywhere but knowing that if it's what she wants, I'll let her.

"Stay."

"Only for you, Crow. Let me go tell them you're awake," she says. She takes a step, our hands releasing each other's. Lyric hesitates before coming back to my side.

"You really scared me, Crow." Leaning down, she presses her lips to my head. "Don't do that to me again." She sighs before pulling away and heading to the door. I close my eyes and swallow hard. Will she be alright when the time comes? Clearly the fucking devil didn't take me once again. I don't know why he's saving me. I don't know why he won't fucking reach into me and take every last piece of my soul. It's already black. There is nothing left of it.

"Glad you're awake, motherfucker." Ruger strolls in looking as happy as ever.

"Somethin' like that," I grumble.

"Fucked your ass up pretty good. I feel like shit, brother. I knew you were off. I wish I didn't let you go off on your own," he says.

That's the first time since I've known Ruger that he has ever said anything like that. The solemn look in his eyes bugs me. What the hell is this girly shit all about? Is there something they aren't telling me?

"What the fuck are you talkin' about, man? You sound like a bitch." I chuckle lightly. My chest is on fire but my head spins. The door opens before he can say anything else. Hawk, Smokey, and Draven walk in with Mayhem of all people.

"If I knew I had to damn near die to see your sorry ass, I would have done it sooner." I smile as Mayhem walks toward the bed.

"Heard that. Came down as soon as I heard about the accident. Wanted to make sure your sorry ass was followin' directions. Dec will be down in a few days. Told Hawk we'd help out with what we can."

I watch Mayhem for a minute. Something seems off with him, too. In fact, the more I look around the room, they all seem off. The door opens again and Lyric walks in with a doctor at her side. She wrings her hands together in front of her, nervously. What the fuck is going on?

"Someone gonna tell me why the fuck you all look like we're headin' to a funeral? Cause it sure as fuck ain't mine." I make the obvious known. Mayhem chuckles but Lyric looks sick to her stomach.

"Lyric? Come here, baby," I tell her. She hesitates and looks around like the other guys might tell her no. My body wants to fight. I can feel it in me. I'm about to say more but she decides to move. She walks over and grabs my hand. I scoot over as far as I can and motion for her to sit.

"What the hell is goin' on?" I growl. Lyric jolts a little before the doctor clears his throat.

"Mr. Marcus, we ran some tests when you came in the other day," he begins. The other day? What the hell?

"How long have I been out?" I ask, looking to Lyric.

"Four days," she says softly. Fuck! I look back to the doctor.

"You have what's called Non-Hodgkins Lymphoma, Mr. Marcus. The treatments can be started as soon as your head is healed up. I want you to be at hundred percent when we start the chemo." Lyric sobs next to me, but all I heard was chemo. What the hell is happening to me?

"What the fuck, doc? I don't know what that shit is," I growl.

"It's a form of cancer, Mr. Marcus. We can do treatments. A minimum of six months. You will spend a lot of time in the hospital. You will need plenty of rest at home as well as-"

"How long?" I cut him off and ask. Fuck his chemo. Fuck his stay in the hospital shit.

"It's hard to say. With treatment we can prolong-"

"No. I don't want it."

"Mr. Marcus-"

"I said I don't fuckin' want it! In fact, get this shit off me so I can get the hell outta here," I roar as I tear at the wires and IVs that lead into my arm. Lyric jumps off the bed, Draven and Ruger taking her place. They pin me to the bed by my shoulders. I look between them with venom lacing my veins.

"Get the fuck off me. I'm leavin'!" I roar once more. They share a glance before moving back. I sit up, my head spinning slightly. I hold still for a second to calm the urge to vomit.

"Baby, hand me my clothes," I tell Lyric, my voice calming slightly. She moves to the little chair in the corner and brings me a pile of clothes, setting them next to me.

"You motherfuckers gonna watch me get naked?" I ask looking at the guys. They all groan and shake their heads before walking out of the room, the doctor behind them.

"You want me to help?" Lyric asks. I look over at her and smile.

"You want to get your hands on me already?" I tease. She just smiles and grabs my shirt.

"Actually, I wanted your hands on me, but since you're the patient, I suppose I can help out."

I laugh a little as she pulls the stickers off my chest. She tosses the wires to the side and pulls my shirt over my head. I stuff my arms in the holes as pain ricochets through my body.

"Fucked my bike up good, huh?" I ask her as she kneels in front of me with my jeans.

"You're lucky you had a helmet. You have a shitty concussion," she says as I stand and she pulls my jeans up my legs. I like watching her like this, so sure of herself. It fits her.

"So, that shit I heard you talkin' to the nurse? It kinda make me hard, darlin'," I tell her watching her cheeks flush.

"She had that coming. She has been a pain in the ass since you got here. She wasn't going to let me in until I told her you were my husband." Lyric stands in front of me stoically. I can tell the news is hurting her but she doesn't let on. She bottles it up like I do and eventually it will break her if she doesn't get it out. I would know. Now isn't the time though.

"You gonna break me outta here, baby?"

"That depends. Can I stay with you a while?" she asks.

"You gonna play naughty nurse?" I ask her, raising an eyebrow. Lyric giggles and my heart melts.

"I think I can do that."

Chapter 12

Healing from the accident has taken a toll on me. I thought I was ready to get my ass back into the swing of life but that concussion kicked my ass. I've been down for a few weeks and it's making me crazy. Too many nights I'd lay awake and wonder why the world hates me the way it does. Why it can't just let me go. I don't understand the hold the universe has on me. Is it a form of torture? It's doing a damn good job if it is.

I roll over and grab the bottle of Jack of the night stand, pushing myself up. If I can't ride, I can still drink and fuck. And fuck I have. I've had Lyric wrapped up in my arms every goddamn night since I've been home. She leaves for a while during the day but she always comes back. We haven't talked about that black eye yet but I hope she doesn't think it's been forgotten. I hear the front door slam as I down another gulp from the bottle. Drinking gives me a slight satisfaction. That and the fact that I know my own body is slowly killing me. The thought of doing the chemo crossed my mind for the briefest of moments. It was only because of her. How fair is that?

"You gonna drink 'til you die, motherfucker?" Draven asks, dropping onto the bed next to me with a joint hanging between his lips.

"Maybe. Who gives a shit anyway?" I ask, taking another drink.

Draven chuckles before he says, "Got some word on Ancients. They haven't set foot near Henley, but from what's gettin' said, they are formin' an alliance with Road Ryders." He inhales before passing me the joint. I take it and take a long hit before passing it back.

"Fuck the Ryders. They aren't shit. One good shot and we take out half their army. Their soldiers are bullshit. So, is their prez. Hope Hawk knows that shit," I tell him. I lay my head back as the world spins around me, the liquor and weed giving me a euphoric feeling.

"Yeah. He wanted you to ride out on that one. Got your bike up and runnin' again," He says. I place my hands behind my head and look at him.

"You did? When?" I ask with a grin.

"Week ago. Figured you'd wanna get back on it." Draven sighs before shoving off the bed. "You want me to tell Hawk you're in?"

I let his question hang in the air for a second before I say, "Fuck yeah. Ain't doin' no good layin' up in the bed." Draven nods with a slight smile on his face. I know I've missed a lot. I know they need me too. The front door closes again as Draven looks over his shoulder. Lyric walks in looking like hell once again.

"You been restin', sweetheart?" Draven asks her. I know they all care about her and it's surprised me how much they have taken to her. They don't treat her like they do most of the girls here. They treat her better, with more respect.

"Yeah," she says, walking past him. I watch her as she digs through the dresser, not saying a word to anyone. My chest tightens. Something is clearly going on in that head of hers.

"I'll talk to you later, Crow."

I nod my head and watch Draven leave before I shove off the bed. I walk up behind Lyric, wrapping my arms around her waist. As soon as I touch her, she sobs. My heart aches for her. I want to do anything in my power to make her smile.

"Talk to me, baby," I whisper against her neck. I can smell the alcohol on her. Is she drunk too?

"I hate life, Crow. I hate everything about it," she cries. I spin her in my arms, looking her in the eye. She looks as lost as she did the first time I

79

saw her in that warehouse, which scares the fuck out of me.

"What happened?" I ask, my tone hardening a little more.

"Luther is a bastard. I wish I never had to go back there," she cries.

"You don't have to. Why the fuck do you still go there, Lyric?" Hearing that she still goes back to that place pisses me off. I knew she went out but I didn't know she'd go home. Is that what happened to her eye? Is that why she comes back looking like shit all the time?

"You don't understand." She grits her teeth and pulls away from me. She walks toward the bed, grabs the bottle of jack, and brings it to her lips. I watch as she takes a long pull, swallowing it down. She's in obvious need of a distraction of her own, and I won't take that away from her.

"I don't understand 'cause you won't tell me!" I snap at her. Her head snaps around, her eyes locking with mine.

"What do you want to know, Crow? Huh? How he used to stick his fingers inside me? How he used to kiss my neck like you just did? That's the only place that's home! I've never had any other home, Crow!" The tears fall down her face but they aren't of sadness. They are tears of hate. I know those tears all too well.

"I'll kill him," I say with my jaw clenched tightly.

"How are you going to do that when you want to die to? Huh? How the fuck, Crow!" she screams. Lyric takes another long pull before throwing the bottle across the room. It slams into the wall next to me, shattering into a million pieces.

"You always knew my end game, Lyric. That never changed," I say softly. She shakes her head before she walks toward the door. I'm pissed. My body is practically vibrating. I want to rip that motherfucker's throat out for even looking at her wrong, but putting his hands on her? Fuck no. Add to that that Lyric is seething with her own rage and anger and I just about can't handle anymore. I want to lose myself with her, but as I stand here thinking on it, I know what I need to do. I know what I need to tell her if we are going to make any kind of sense out of this relationship we have going on.

"Don't you walk out of here!" I roar. Lyric stops and turns to look at me. She laughs. Out of nowhere she starts angrily laughing.

"What do you want from me, Crow?" she screams, throwing her arms out to the sides. She's so damn beautiful. So damn perfect. I want so much from her but I can't have it.

"Wait here," I tell her, grinding my teeth painfully together. I suppose if we are being real right now, I might as well be real with her. I need her to know why my life will never amount to anything. I need her to know the whole fucking story of why I need this life to end. She has to understand me.

I walk into the bathroom and grab the razor from under the sink. In an angry drunken haze, I plug it in and start cutting off all my hair. Lyric rushes into the bathroom, her mouth hanging open.

"What are you doing?" she yells as she watches all my shaggy brown hair fall to the floor.

"I'm showin' you. I'm showin' you why I'm not meant to be here. I'm showin' you how the world has turned on me and it's slowly suckin' the life from me. It's taken all I have to live this long, Lyric. I need you to know why! I need you to know so that you can move on with your life without me one day!" I keep shaving until all my hair is gone. I look up in the mirror, setting the razor on the sink. I cock my head to the side, studying myself in the mirror.

"Where did you get that scar on your head?" she asks softly, moving to touch it. Slowly running the tips of her fingers over the length, tears fall down my face.

"One night. Four minutes. That's all it took, Lyric. Four minutes."

Chapter 13

Lyric grabs my hand, leading me from the bathroom. Once we're in the bedroom, she pulls my shirt over my head, brushing off the hair that's fallen on my skin. She takes her time, making sure my body is cleaned. Next, she removes my jeans, and I let her. Kicking them to the side, I sit on the edge of the bed in my boxers. My chest aches. My heart feels as if it's being ripped out of my chest.

"I was with this girl once. I didn't love her. Hell, I didn't like her much. We weren't even really together. We fucked and that was it. She got pregnant. Never wanted kids. I wasn't sure I did either. But when the nurse passed me that little boy bundled in a blanket, my heart melted. He was seven pounds of perfection. Looked just like me. Even had my eyes." Sighing, I take a breath and continue. I need to get this out. "Beth didn't want him. She never did. She took off right when she got out of the hospital. Left me with a son that I had no idea how to care for. I did it, though. I learned how to take care of him by myself. He was everything to me. He became my world, and there was nothin' I wouldn't do for him."

"Did the guys help?" Lyric asks softly.

I nod solemnly. "As much as I'd let them. He was my boy, I wanted to be the one carin' for him. I did the best I could. He was happy. I was happy. We were our own little family... One day when Gabe was six, Beth showed up at the park we were at. She had a bunch of guys with her. Wasn't a lot I could do one on seven. She was messed up, high outta her mind. They weren't far behind; their eyes were wild with whatever they were usin'. There was this one guy that was really disturbin'. Every time he'd look at me or Gabe, somethin' in me wanted to snap. My heart was beatin' so fast, ready to explode when they grabbed us both. Took us to an old warehouse. Nobody said a whole lot and it made me worry. The silence was eerie. I had a split second to text Ruger and let him know what was goin' down. I held Gabe close to me when the guy pulled a gun and pointed it right at me. Beth yelled about how it was my fault she had to do this. How that boy meant more to me than her. I hadn't seen her in years. Didn't even know she was alive," I rasp, tears continuously flowing down my cheeks as I talk.

"Crow, you don't have to do this," Lyric says.

Looking over, I motion for her to come to me. I scoot into the middle of the bed, my back resting against the headboard. Lyric straddles me, sitting in my lap, facing me as I continue. "One of the other guys came and ripped Gabe from my embrace. I fought like hell. Punched, kicked, screamed - you name it. I fought to keep him in my arms. I told him everything was gonna be okay. I tried to calm him as he cried across the dingy room. The sick one, the one with gun passed it to another. They traded off. My son for the weapon. He held Gabe around the neck with this look in his eyes, like the devil himself. I saw it. I saw it all. He squeezed Gabe's throat…" A sob rips my insides out. I can't breathe. Forcing myself to take a few deep breaths I try to regain enough strength to finish this once and for all.

"Crow, stop," Lyric begs with tears of her own. Redness rimming her beautiful eyes.

"I moved to go after him when the gun fired. I was thrown back. I hit the floor hard and my right eye was covered in blood. I couldn't see what was happenin'. I moved the best I could, but the pain in my head wouldn't let me get up. I fought, Lyric. Fuck, I tried to fight. I heard the gasps. I tried to shake the blood out of my face…and then I saw him. His lifeless eyes. That monster killed him, Lyric. That monster killed my son, right in front of me for no fuckin' reason. His eyes will always haunt me. Those dark brown eyes that fill every goddamn nightmare I have. I looked into his eyes, Lyric. I saw the pleadin' in them. The wonderin' why his daddy was lettin' this shit happen to him. He was silently beggin' me with his eyes, but I heard him. His little voice. He sobbed the word daddy. That bastard didn't care. He took his time. Tortured him. Made him breathe life back into his lungs before takin' it away again." I lose it then. I break down and there is nothing I can do to stop. My world crumbles at my feet. My heart feels dead. There's nothing left inside of me now. Lyric has it all... Every ounce of me in the palm of her hand.

Wrapping her arms around me, she holds on tight, siphoning the pain from my soul into her own. I cry on her shoulder until I can barely breathe any longer. I cry until there's nothing left. Her tender hand roams up and down my back as I finish unleashing years of pain.

"I'm so sorry, Crow. So sorry," she says gently against my ear. Her breath dances over my skin. As the tears slowly subside, I nuzzle her neck. The soft skin that smells like strawberries. I kiss her gently, her body responding. "Crow," she says, her voice littered with pain.

"Tell me, Lyric. Tell me what he did to you. I wanna make it all go away," I tell her with pure heart and honesty.

"He would touch me. Tell me it was my fault. He would say that I had to learn. Learn how to be a woman. I was always bigger than the other kids. All through school he would tell me that no one would love me. No one would like me. I was too fat to get a boyfriend. He would hit me to make me understand how ugly I was. I always believed him. He hurt me in ways that no child should be hurt." She cries on my shoulder, her warm tears falling down my skin.

"He lied to you, Lyric," I say as my own tears begin to dry.

"About what?"

"Someone lovin' you. I love you, Lyric. More than a man should for just meetin' a woman. More than I should for what I'm gonna do with my life. I do though."

"You have done so much for me, Crow. I've never met anyone like you. You don't see the me on the outside. You always see me, the me on the inside. I've never felt like this before," she cries.

"Promise me that you will move on. Promise me that you will spend the rest of my time with me but then you do somethin' bigger," I beg her. Lyric leans back, looking in my eyes.

"Bigger?" She wiggles a little to tease me breaking the heartbroken memories of our past. I smile and kiss her gently.

"You'll be doin' a lot of that, baby. But I mean it. I need to know that you can do this, Lyric."

Lyric cups my face in her hands before she says, "For you, Crow. I can do anything for you."

Chapter 14

"Where are you going?" I glance over when I hear her groggy voice. Lyric lays there with her hair a mussed-up mess, her cheeks bright. She's gorgeous.

"Got a run today with the guys," I tell her. She watches me walk through the room in nothing but a towel.

"Is that a good idea?" she asks. I blow out a breath before turning and walking back to the bed. Sitting on the edge, I run my hand over my head.

"It's my life, Lyric. I need to get back into what I do. Today isn't my day, darlin'. I promise."

Looking over my shoulder at her, she smiles. Fuck it. I have time for another round with her before I leave. I stand up and lose the towel, dropping it to the floor. When I kneel on the bed, Lyric licks those lips of hers. I crawl over to her, looming over her body before kissing her. Today is the day. I'm getting her out of these goddamn t-shirts if it's the last thing I do on this earth. I run my tongue down her neck, feeling her tremble beneath me. I nip at her shoulder before pulling back and looking down at her.

"I'm takin' this off," I tell her as I tug at her shirt.

She looks at me with pain in her eyes but I don't let that stop me. Not today. I hold my hands out to her, waiting for her to take them. I want her to be able to do this with me. Take this step in the right direction with me. I almost lose my shit when she actually takes my hands and sits up. I grin as I reach for the hem of her shirt, slowing pulling it over her head.

"Do you really have to do it so slow, Crow?" she snaps at me. I chuckle.

"Gettin' greedy, are you?" I tease her before pulling it all the way off and tossing it to the side. I like that she only sleeps in the shirt now. I'd prefer she sleeps in nothing but we're making baby steps to that. As I push her back on the bed, my heart leaps in my chest. This woman has come so far in such a short time. I love seeing her come into her element. I love seeing her reach for her goals, and this was one that I wanted for her.

"Smokey said he has a surprise for you later," I tell her before kissing her.

"What surprise?" she asks, seeming as confused as I am.

I shrug before I reach between us grabbing my dick. I tease her entrance before I slip inside of her with a groan.

"He didn't say. Fuck, Lyric." I groan in pleasure. Sliding in and out of her feels like heaven. Lyric wraps her hands around my back, holding me closer to her. My lips trail a line down her neck, loving the way she shudders beneath me. When I sit up, I look in her eyes and all I can see is love. Lyric holds a lot inside of her, but I can tell that when she loves something, she goes all in. I can't help but grin at her as I thrust harder. Her eyes roll back, pleasure painting that perfect face of hers. That's all I ever want to see on her. Happiness. I know she's capable of so much more than she thinks she is and she deserves every bit of it.

"You're so beautiful." Whispering the words, I didn't think she heard me, but her eyes open and catch on mine. The air rushes from my lungs as I pick up my pace. I thrust roughly into her as she screams my name. My heart swells with love. If only things were different. If I were different, I could picture myself happy with her. I would want that with her but I'm me and that will never change. I come inside of her and lower my head to kiss her once more as she catches her breath.

"Promise me you won't leave here tonight." Whatever the hell is happening with her stepdad I don't want her around it. I want her safe.

"I won't but I will have to one day," she says almost sadly.

"No. This is your place now. No matter what happens with me, this is home, Lyric. You never have to worry about him again," I tell her as I kiss the side of her face. I nuzzle into her neck and inhale the scent of her. She calms me. I love that about her, but there are just some things that not even love can take away. There is a pain that is etched deep inside of me that not even she can remove.

I'm enjoying my spot in her neck when someone pounds on the door. Lyric giggles and I pull back to kiss her one more time.

"Suppose I should hurry up." One more kiss and I pull out of her and climb off the bed. Lyric sighs as I grab my clothes.

"Why are you so perfect? Even your ass is perfect," she mumbles behind me, making me laugh.

I pull my boxers and my jeans on before I turn to look at her. Buttoning my jeans, I grin and say, "Clearly you haven't looked at your ass lately.

I wanna bite into it." Giving her a wink, I sit on the edge of the bed to pull my socks and boots on. The bed shifts and Lyric's fingers slowly move over my back. The bumps that form on my skin make her laugh. She loves doing that to me.

"You're makin' it harder for me to leave." Just as the words leave my mouth, someone pounds on the door again. Lyric giggles once more before I feel her lips press into my back between my shoulder blades.

"Come back," she whispers. Those words will haunt me forever.

"This time," I say before standing and grabbing my shirt. When I'm fully dressed, I grab my phone and cigarettes and head out. I can't turn back to look at her. I can't see that look in her eyes. Hurting Lyric was never part of my plan. Finding her again wasn't either, but now that she's here I feel selfish. We all know I'm dying. It's just a matter of time now but I knew this long before the cancer was found. So why do I feel like I need to keep her just a little longer? Why do I want to make her feel special when all I'm going to do is rip that away from her when I'm gone? As I throw the door open, Ruger stands there with a shit eating grin on his face.

"What?"

"You gettin' some pussy?" he asks.

"Fuck off. Don't you have a woman?" I shove past him and light up a cigarette.

"Smokin' will give you cancer," he laughs hysterically. I can't help but laugh with him.

"Think we're beyond that now, don't you?" Glancing over at him, his laughter slowly fades. Ruger is one hell of a man but I can see the soft parts in him. His brothers are his weakness.

"Don't do that, Ruger. We're good, brother. I just wanna live until I decide it's time." He cocks his head to the side and studies me for a long minute.

"Ain't give up the idea yet, huh?" he asks, his smile long since faded.

"Nope. I want a little bit more and I'm good. You don't get it, man. The way I see his eyes at night. The way I can hear him say daddy. It's too much."

Ruger slaps a hand on my shoulder but doesn't say anything else. He knows where my head goes and he's always known the end plan. It was never a secret kept from any of the guys.

"Let's do this. I wanna make someone bleed."

Chapter 15

The ride is sweet. I've missed my bike. There's something about being on it and on the open road that hits you right in the soul. Your body and mind work together for once and it frees you in a way. That's what I feel every time I'm on it.

Following Ruger off the exit, my body tenses slightly. That's never a good feeling to have when you know something might go down. I shake it off and keep my head right as we turn down a side road. The air feels thicker the closer we get. That's a sign in itself. We know what we're doing. That feeling is *how* we know. Ruger pulls to a stop with Draven and me right behind him. I watch him climb off, setting his helmet on the seat.

"A block and half down is their meetin' point. They don't have a clubhouse." He chuckles when he says that. I knew they didn't. Most of them little pricks don't even own Harleys; they opt for crotch rockets. To me, that doesn't even make them a club worth having.

"Hope they don't want a street race," I add with a chuckle of my own.

Draven pulls his guns out of his saddlebags and starts stuffing them into the back of his jeans when he says, "I'm up for a race. Doubt they'll get that far though," he says holding up one of his guns, and just I shake my head.

"Heard that. What's the plan here, Ruger? We taken them all out?" I ask, checking my own guns before shoving them into the waistband of my pants. Pulling my t-shirt down over them, I look back up at Ruger.

"Take what you want, brother. Ancients ain't havin' them!" Draven says as I laugh.

"Guess that's a yes?" I ask him. Draven nods his head laughing.

"Take what we want. It's all fair game. Too bad I didn't know that at the time, I would have brought the truck and brought a few home for the party," Ruger adds.

Draven laughs as he double checks he has everything. I do the same. When we're all ready, we walk down the road like we own it. Doesn't matter that those little shits are just down the street. Doesn't matter that they are forming an alliance with someone else. All that matters is that we know we are bigger and better than they are. We know that in the matter of a few phone calls we could burn this neighborhood to the ground.

"Which house?" I ask when Ruger starts to slow down.

With a nod he says, "That one."

I look over to where he's looking and see one bike in the front yard. I know there's more though. Always are. "Shit. I'm takin' the back. You know the bikes are back there. I'm about to fuck them up," I say with a grin.

Draven chuckles and adds, "That makes two of us. If they run, it'll be to those bikes and I want an upfront view."

"Bitches. Leave the big man to go in, huh?" Ruger utters. Draven and I both turn to look at him before he chuckles and says, "Don't let any get away. I don't feel much like runnin' today." I run my hand over my face and shake my head. That man is insane.

I pull one of my guns and move toward the back of the house. We aren't hiding or trying to go in unseen either. We don't give a shit if they see us. Hopping the little back fence, Draven follows my lead. I lean against the fence, pulling a cigarette out and lighting it up.

"Look at all that shit," I say pointing to their bikes. There are ten of them parked in a little row. It's almost too perfect to shoot up. Almost.

"How sweet. You think they have assigned parkin'?" Draven asks making me laugh.

"Looks like it." Just as I blow out a ring of smoke, someone opens the back door. I tilt my head to the side and watch the kid. His eyes blaze with fire as if he knew what we were doing here. No way in fuck he knows but I like the look. That means we're going to have a good time with him.

"Hey, pretty boy! Which one's yours?" I holler at him making Draven laugh.

"Who the fuck do you think you are coming here?" he roars. I shrug my shoulder before taking another hit from my cigarette.

"Wanted to see your pretty bikes," I say with a smirk. Smoke rolls through my nose. I see the kid make a hand signal inside before two more come to the door behind him.

"Now we got a party," Draven says.

I hold my gun in one hand, pointing at the bikes and ask, "Well? Which is it?" The asshole doesn't answer so I fire a shot into the tire of the closest one.

"You want a war?" Another behind him yells before I see a gun. I tap Draven on the shoulder and motion for him to look. He laughs.

We don't move from our positions on the fence. Not until my smoke is gone. I flick it to the ground, shoving off the fence as the one with the gun stands in the doorway watching. I can tell you for sure if someone fired at my bike, I would have already shot.

"Heard anything about the Ancients lately?" I ask as Draven and I advance. That draws their attention. A shot comes out of nowhere, grazing my arm. I look down at it before Draven turns and fires. All hell breaks loose then.

Shots ring through the air. Some barely missing me. I fire and take out all of the bikes while Draven takes out the drivers. I can hear screams coming from inside so I know Ruger has made his way in. When the firing stops, I'm out of breath and tired. Doc told me I'd feel like this but this is too much. I thought at first it was adrenaline but I feel like I could sleep for days. Too much happening at once has really been wearing me out and I don't fucking like that feeling.

"You good?" Ruger comes out of the back door and looks at me. I shake my head. I walk over slowly and lean against the side of the house.

"You hit?" Ruger asks moving toward me.

"Just grazed. I'm just tired. Feel like fallin' asleep right here," I tell him.

"Well, they're all dead. You can take a nap before we leave." I cock my head to the side and look up at him. He stands there looking as serious as ever.

"You want me to take a nap amongst all the dead bodies?" I ask him just to be clear.

"They're dead, brother. Ain't none of them gonna bother you." I close my eyes and wonder what the hell goes on in that man's head.

"It's daylight, man. We need to move out before someone calls this shit in," I remind him. Ruger shrugs and walks back inside.

"Can you believe that shit?" I look to Draven.

"Come on. You can ride bitch. I'll drive you home." Draven walks up and throws his arm around me. I damn near knock his teeth down his throat.

"I'd rather die, asshole."

Chapter 16

A nap. Who the fuck would have known a grown ass man would need a nap like a kid. I feel like the world is sitting on my shoulders though. The heaviness inside of me is overwhelming. I dropped onto the bed as soon as we got back. Lyric was over at Smokey's with Bray so she didn't see how I looked when I came in. I'm glad for that. I know she would have a fucking fit if she saw me. I saw myself in the mirror and couldn't believe it was really me. I hate that this feeling is all I have now. I hate that I can't be stronger or at least as strong as I know I am. The bed shifts next to me when I turn my head and see her. Looking like pure perfection as always.

"You've been asleep for a long time," she says, the look of concern covering her face. I stuff my face back into the pillow and groan.

"Just tired is all," I mumble when I feel her hand on my back.

"Just tired, huh? You slept for two days, Crow."

What the fuck did she just say? I pull myself up and look around the room a little stunned.

There's no way in hell that I slept for two days. How the hell can that happen?

"You're jokin' right?" I look back at Lyric.

She shakes her head slowly before looking away and saying, "I was going to wake you up, but then we talked to the doctor. He said to let you sleep. That your body needed it." I scoot closer to her, wrapping my hand around the back of her neck, pulling her face to mine.

"You know what my body needs?" I ask her before running my tongue over her bottom lip.

"No."

"Yeah, you do. It needs you." Kissing her roughly, she moans into my mouth. I've missed hearing that from her. I've missed her. Even in my dreams a part of me ached for her. I don't know how that's even possible but I felt it.

"Not right now. Smokey is waiting," she says breathlessly.

"Since when do I give a shit?" I ask before kissing her again. Lyric wiggles on the bed, no doubt wet right now. I know she wants this but then something else hits me. Shit! I slept through the surprise.

"Fuck. Your surprise," I say when I pull back. A moment of dread skates through my stomach before she smiles.

"That's what he's waiting for. He said he didn't want to do it unless you were there. No one will tell me what the hell is going on," she says, looking a little pissed. It does my heart good to see her like that. You would think I would want her to smile but that scowl on her face makes my heart leap. I like when she's on edge. She's vulnerable which is something she doesn't let her self be anymore.

"I'm glad he waited. I wanna see the look on your face. Come on." Without thinking about it anymore I climb off the bed and grab her hand. Lyric tries to protest by pulling back but I just yank her ass off the bed anyway.

"Got a little attitude today?" I ask with a wink.

"No. I just don't like surprises, Crow."

As I drag her down the hallway I remember all the nights we've talked. The first night her stepdad came into her room he told her he had a surprise for her. That surprise was him hurting her. I close my eyes and let out a breath before I turn to look at her.

"I'm sorry. I didn't even think about it. Fuck, Lyric." She shakes her head, pulling me against her. I love when she does this - gives me a part of her.

"Not your fault. I know this isn't the same thing. It's just hard sometimes to deal with it all," she says softly. I know how that feeling is. I deal with it every day.

"The guys love you, Lyric. They might be assholes for the most part, but they do care about you. They wouldn't do anything to hurt you," I remind her. She nods her head. Placing a kiss to her forehead, I grab her hand and head for the door.

"You don't want to eat or something first?" she asks sounding concerned about me. My heart beats double time knowing she really cares about me.

"Hell no. I'll eat you later."

Pulling Lyric out into the night air, I'm hit with reality. A reality that I've wanted so badly but can never keep. My reality with Lyric is easy. I can make her trust. I can make her love. Show her what it means to be loved and then when I'm gone, she will have all those tools at her fingertips to move on with her life and leave her past where it belongs. She will be able to accomplish things that I couldn't.

As we walk toward the clubhouse with our hands intertwined, a sadness washes over me. I would have loved to stay with her. Show her how much she means to me for the rest of my life, but the world has other plans for me. I can't say that I'm sorry for what I'll do when the time comes because I'm not. Gabe, my son, is out there waiting for me somewhere.

"Are you okay?" Lyric pulls my attention from those thoughts to her. Tilting my head to the side, I smile.

"Perfect." Because I am. Right now I'm fucking perfect. She makes me perfect. But in time, that will fade too.

Chapter 17

We step into the clubhouse and the amount of people inside surprises me. Everyone is here. Even the Northern Chapter of Bastards are roaming around.

"Look at who finally decided to wake the fuck up. I told your girl I'd come sneak into bed with you and shit. She didn't think that was a good idea," Mayhem says before pulling me into a hug.

"You did that and Taylor would kill me. I would cut your dick off, man." Mayhem pulls back smiling as he looks at me.

"You look good, brother. Feelin' okay?" he asks. I nod my head. Glancing around I see Declan and Tic. Makes me happy to have all the guys in one spot. We may be different but we are all brothers.

"Let's get this shit goin'," Smokey yells from somewhere behind me. I turn around and watch him walk to the middle of the room with some man in a suit. He looks completely out of place unless he's a lawyer. Oh, shit! Is he a lawyer?

"What the fuck is that?" I nod at the guy as I talk to Mayhem.

"That's one of those city boys. Ain't he pretty?" he chuckles. I slap my hand across his chest as the room grows silent. Smokey stands proudly with his head held high. I have no fucking idea what he's doing and I'm a little nervous.

"Most of you know what's happenin' here tonight. Some don't. Mainly Crow and his old lady." Smokey chuckles while Lyric squeezes my hand tighter. "Not long ago, Lyric came into this clubhouse and got drunk off her ass. It was interestin' to say the least." Everyone laughs but Lyric tenses. I release her hand and wrap it around her waist instead, pulling her into my side.

"She did somethin' most of the girls around here wouldn't. She grabbed a microphone and sang her fuckin' heart out. She killed it. We all heard it. After talkin' to Crow about it, I knew what needed to be done. This is James Michael. He's with a show called America Sing. You got an audition darlin'." Smokey looks at Lyric as he says the words.

Her body becomes tenser in my arms. The smile that spreads across my face is genuine and shocked. I can't believe he did this. He did ask me about her singing. I told him that she really wanted to do it like her mom. I just never saw this coming. I pull Lyric in front of me as the room explodes in cheers. Her eyes dance over my face as she shakes her head.

"I can't do it," she says softly. I grab her face in my hands and force her to look me in the eye.

"You can do it. You were born to do it. I've heard you, baby. That voice is magical. You wanted this for a long time, Lyric. Here's your chance, baby. You can do this," I tell her honestly. Lyric chews her lips before I lean in and kiss her. She doesn't fight me and everyone in the room is still cheering.

When I pull away from her she looks worried but then says, "Will you do it with me?" My heart spirals out of control. She wants me with her to do this? I'll damn sure see her through it.

"You know it." Her face lights up when she throws her arms around me. I hold her tightly, whispering in her ear, "You can do anything, Lyric. Your heart is pure." I hear her sniffle but I don't move to let her go just yet. I want to hold onto her for as long as I can.

"Alright, let her breathe." Draven's voice breaks the moment. I pull back reluctantly and wipe her eyes. We both look at the man standing next to him.

"James Michael. I've heard a lot about you, Lyric." The man extends his hand to her. Lyric takes it in her shaky one.

"I watched your shows when I was younger. I never once dreamt I'd be on it," she says with a nervous laugh.

"Auditions are in two weeks. I'd like for you to come down and show us what you can do."

Lyric looks to me as I grin. I nod my head once telling her I'll still be around for her in those two weeks.

"That would be fantastic. I don't know how to thank you," she says.

James looks over his shoulder at Smokey and says, "You can thank him. We were good friends a long time ago. He saved my ass from a life I wasn't ready for. He's a good guy. I'll see you in two weeks." Shaking her hand once more, James turns on his heel and walks away. We all watch as he makes his way out of the clubhouse. My heart is pounding in my chest. I know this has to mean so much to Lyric. When she finally turns to look at me, I can see the smile in her eyes.

"You excited?" I ask her smiling with her.

"Did you know?"

Shaking my head no, I tell her, "No. Not a fuckin' clue but I know you can do this, Lyric. Whatever you need to get ready, I got you." Lyric grabs me and kisses me roughly. I slide my arms around her waist, pulling her against me. Grabbing a handful of her ass, I groan into her mouth. Fuck, I love this woman and every single curve on her.

"Enough of that! It's a party. We're celebratin'!" Smokey roars from behind us. Lyric pulls back and turns to face him. His eyes sparkle in the light. I've never seen him look like this before. He looks fucking happy and it scares the shit out of me.

"I don't know how to thank you," she says stepping into his waiting arms. I watch them hug before Bray pulls Lyric away from him and hugging her.

"Why?" I ask Smokey as my eyes travel the room with Lyric.

"She deserves it. You deserve it. I don't fuckin' know, man. I see how you light up when she's here. I see the way you look at her. I know your plans haven't changed but mine have. I want more for this club than death all the goddamn time. I figured I'd start with Lyric." His words mean more to me than he could ever know.

"That's all I want for her too. Somethin' good in her life. Somethin' she can accomplish." My eyes never leave her as I talk. She smiles and laughs, hugging the other girls. My heart swells with love and pride for that woman.

Chapter 18

The parties in full swing. Lyric hasn't smiled this much since I met her. That day still sits freshly in my mind too. The warehouse. The look in her eyes. The hurt. I hated it even then. I still do. The one thing I am thankful for is changing it slightly. I know she still holds a lot inside but I can see the shift in her. She's stronger than she was. I like to think I had a hand in that. I light up a cigarette and watch her body move as she dances with Bray and Brooke. She's happy, that's all I can keep thinking.

"She seems like a good one." Declan leans against the wall with his arms crossed over his chest, smiling in her direction.

"Yeah, she is. She's gonna do things in her life," I tell him.

"Things ain't been easy on you lately. Anything I can do to help?" I pull my eyes from my girl and look over at him.

"No. I got things handled. Shit happens, yeah? We move on like always." I blow the smoke from my cigarette through my nose as he nods his head.

"Heard that. Just know I'm around." I watch Declan walk over to his woman, pulling her into his arms. Glancing around the room, I watch the guys all drink, laugh, and have a good time. It's these moments I want to take with me. These are the ones I want to remember forever. This is my family and there is nothing more satisfying than seeing your family happy together.

"Ancients aren't really happy with what happened to their little bitches." I chuckle before looking over at Hawk. The smile on his face says he is though.

"I bet not. They won't be ridin' around on those little crotch rockets anymore. I don't get what they needed them for anyway," I say being honest. I've thought it over while I've been standing here. Hell, I thought about when we were shooting the shit out of them.

"You think it was for cover?" Hawk asks me. Shrugging my shoulder, I pull my cigarette back to my lips.

"Hard to say. They weren't much of anything to be honest. They were just there. Keep us on edge, maybe?" Hawk shakes his head, running has hand through his hair, tugging slightly. That's always a sign that he is getting frustrated with a situation.

"Don't fuckin' know. I know Henley is catchin' some shit down his way but it's mainly from pigs. I don't know how any of that plays into this shit though. Doesn't make sense." Taking the cigarette from my hand, he brings it to his lips. I smile and shake my head.

"No it don't. What if those pretty boys were in with some dirty cops? Seen that shit more than I care to admit," I add. Hawk blows the smoke from his lungs, letting his mind wander.

"It's possible. Ain't like they haven't shown their dirty asses around here before. Why Henley, though? They don't run nearly enough shit to be targeted. And for what advantage? Ancients ain't shit. We all know it. Hell, they know!" he says a little louder as his nerves begin to set in.

"What if it wasn't Ancients?" I ask pulling his glare to mine.

"What do you mean?"

"What if Ancients are just a ploy. A set up. We fucked one of their so-called alliances without a goddamn blink of an eye. We weren't careful about it. We walked the fuck up there in daylight, for fuck's sake." The more I talk, the more I wonder about that shit myself. We didn't take any precautions. We went in, we killed, we walked the fuck out.

"Goddamn it! You might be right. Fuck!" he growls.

"Still don't add up to Henley. He isn't movin' shit right now. Not after that last hit. Pigs shouldn't have shit on him."

"Ancients might be feedin' them shit. We need to get with Henley. Set up a false run." I grin at that idea.

"Fuck yeah. That's what I'm talkin' about!"

"You in?" Hawk eyes me as I laugh.

"What the fuck, Prez? Of course, I'm in. Who the fuck do you think runs the best goddamn set up runs around here?" I point to myself to make my point. Hawk laughs before slapping a hand on my shoulder.

"You're goddamn right about that! You pick who you want in on it. I'd leave Big and Ricky off it though. Those two have enough real charges on their asses to be hit up with anything else." I nod my head. I already know that.

"I'll take Ruger and a few prospects. They can handle shit. It's about time we threw somethin' their way." Hawk nods his head.

"You just wanna see which one will piss his pants first." I can't help but laugh at that.

"Goddamn right I do!" Hawk laughs and walks away as I smile. Things are looking better around here. I'm glad the guys aren't treating me any different.

"You okay?" Her voice sends chills up my spine but I'm sick of hearing those words spoken to me.

"Can we make a deal?" I ask her, wrapping my hands around her waist. Lyric nods her head with a smile. "No more askin' if I'm okay. If I feel tired or some shit, I'll tell you."

"What do I get in return?" she questions me with a sparkle in those big blue eyes.

"What do you want?"

"You. I want you, Crow."

"You've had me. From the day I saw you in the shadows. You know I couldn't stop thinkin' about you? I wondered where you went. What you were thinkin'. If you were thinkin' about me." Lyric lays her head on my chest, snuggling into me.

"I thought about you a lot. I wondered if you did it when you woke up. If you decided it was best or if you went home. When I saw you at the diner, my heart stopped for a second. I thought I saw a ghost but you were real. You still are real. To me, you always will be." Holding her tighter, I nuzzle my face into her hair. One thing I want to remember about Lyric is this. The way she holds me like I'm her fucking savior when all I can think about is how I'm going to ruin her. A piece of my heart wants to stop with the thoughts of death. It wants to hold onto what I have with her. If I don't do it though, the cancer will.

Or will it?

Chapter 19

"What is this?" I ask Lyric as she drags me along to a million different stores.

"I need something to wear, Crow. I can't just go into that audition in what I have." She stomps.

"And you think I'm lettin' you wear this?" I pick up the half a pair of shorts on the rack in front of me, holding them up to her.

"Hell no! I wouldn't fit my ass in those anyway!" she snaps. Here we go again. "In fact, we need to leave this store. I'm too fat for all of these clothes." That's enough of that. I grab her hand under her protest and drag her toward the back of the store. I catch some stares but I throw them back before I hit the dressing room. Of course, Lyric protests the whole damn way.

"What are you doing, Crow?" she asks when I spin her around and make her face the wall.

"I've had enough of your whinin' shit. I'm too fat. I can't wear that. It's fuckin' annoyin' as hell, Lyric. I thought we moved past that goddamn stage," I say as I bring my hand up. Lyric looks over her shoulder at me, her eyes wide before I slap my hand across her ass.

"Are you really fucking spanking me right now, Crow?" she squeals.

"Goddamn right I am." Another slap on the ass and she yelps.

"We're in a store!" she scream-whispers. I laugh and bring my hand down again. Fuck who can hear me doing this. She needs a little lesson in self-esteem and I'm here to give it to her.

"I don't give a shit. Say 'I'm Lyric and I'm perfect'."

Her eyes meet mine. Look at her trying to avoid it. Another slap.

"Damn it, Crow!"

"Is everything alright back here?" A woman's voice drifts through the dressing room. I keep one hand planted on Lyric's back, keeping her in place while I glare over the door at her. Giving her a smile I nod, "Just teachin' my girl a lesson in self-esteem. Could you go find a dress in an extra extra large please. Somethin' sexy as sin. Make that two dresses. Thanks, darlin'." I give the woman a wink and watch her cheeks blush before she turns and walks away.

"Crow! I can't even believe you did that!" Lyric roars. It's cute.

"Say it, Lyric!" I warn her once more. I think she likes being defiant with me. I think she likes getting spanked in the dressing room. Sliding my hands around to the front of her jeans, I flip the button. Then I unzip them, sliding my hand inside to find her soaking wet.

"Spankin' you in public makes you hot?" I ask her. She tries to move but I hold her in place. I pull my hand free before shoving her jeans to the floor. When I see the thong I bought her, my dick jerks.

"Goddamn!" I growl. I run my hands over her soft ass before slapping it again. Yep, bare ass feels better than through jeans.

"Say it," I tell her once more. I lean down letting my tongue trail over the mounds that are now pink from my hand.

"I'm Lyric," she moans.

"And?" I tease her pussy through the wetness of her panties.

"I'm perfect."

Moaning against her skin, "You're goddamn right you are." I slip a finger inside her panties and toy with her clit. The way she arches has my dick straining to be free. The more I twirl my finger around, the harder I get and the closer she gets.

"Crow." My name leaving her lips is perfection. I stroke her harder wanting her to be on edge. I want her ready to explode.

"I found some dresses." That voice comes back. I pull my finger away from Lyric and she gasps. I reach over the door and wait for the dresses.

"Sir, this is a women's fitting room," she reminds me like I give a shit.

"Yeah, she needs help though. She can't be trusted alone," I say grabbing the dresses. Pulling them back over the door, I can hear her shoes clicking as she walks away.

"Thank fuck I didn't have to fight her," I mumble. Lyric is in the same position that she was in when I left her on the edge of her orgasm. "What's wrong, baby?" She stands up straight and spins to look at me. I can see just how flushed she is. It makes me hard but she will learn to stop talking down about herself. I can't stand that shit.

"That's wrong." She points at me but I just smile.

"Try this on." I pass her a dress. Lyric takes it but looks pissy. I can't help but chuckle at her.

"Why do I need two anyway?"

I watch her pull her shirt over her head. Reaching down I adjust my dick in my jeans. That fucker is grinding painfully against the zipper.

"I hope that hurts," she says nodding toward my dick.

"It won't be later," I reply. I watch her pull the purple dress on and my heart nearly stops. My mouth hangs open and air escapes my lungs.

"You are so fuckin' gorgeous." Lyric doesn't look at me. She looks down at herself. I move to stand behind her, showing her herself in the mirror.

"Look," I say when she doesn't want to look up.

"Those long fuckin' legs. Fuck." I groan once more.

"Do you really think I'm pretty, Crow?"

Our eyes meet in the mirror. Mine full of lust, hers full of a painful past. A past that has made her see herself as fat and ugly not strong and beautiful.

123

"Have I ever lied to you, Lyric? Have I ever given you a reason to think you aren't the most beautiful, sexy women in the world?" My question is honest. I want to know if I've ever made her feel bad about herself.

"No."

"Then it's the truth. I don't think I've met anyone in my life who has captured me the way you do. It isn't just your looks, baby. It's your heart. Someone has stomped it into the ground but you picked it up and put it back together. Look at yourself, Lyric. Really look." Her eyes roam over her body before she stares into the reflection of her own eyes. Slowly, her features soften as she gets a good look at herself.

"You always make me feel good about myself. How did I get so lucky to find you?" A tear slides down her cheek. Reaching around, I wipe it away before kissing her neck.

"I'm the lucky one. You have given me the best time of my life bein' with me, Lyric. I never thought I'd have a reason to want to wake up another day. You do that to me." Kissing her neck once more, she clears her throat and straightens her spine. I stand behind her, watching her in the mirror.

"I'm Lyric and I'm perfect," she says melting my heart. A smile pulls across my face so big it scares me.

"That's my girl!"

Chapter 20

"You never told me why I needed two dresses," Lyric says as we make our way back to the clubhouse, our hands held tightly together.

"Oh, I didn't?" I tease.

"Crow. You know you didn't," she says, bumping me with her shoulder.

"Two things, Lyric. One is gonna be harder for me but I feel like I need to do it with you. The other, it's easy," I tell her. She doesn't get it but I like keeping her on edge.

"We're goin' out tonight. No motorcycle. No cut. No self-doubt. We are gonna have a great night, just me and you. Then I wanna take you somewhere special to me. You good with that?" I look over and her smile is huge.

"No cut? You mean you are dressing up?" she asks, making me laugh.

"Somethin' like that. First we need to talk with Hawk. There's somethin' I need to take care of but I need you there to do it, yeah?" Her smile is gutting me. She holds so much power over me and she doesn't even realize it.

"Ok. I'll do anything you want if I can see you dressed up." She laughs. Fuck, that laugh is the best thing I've ever heard in my life.

"Remember that later when I'm fuckin' the songs right out of you." We both laugh as we step inside. The clubhouse is pretty quiet but it is still early in the day. Not many are hanging out around here at this time. I walk us down the hallway and knock on Hawk's door.

"Yeah, come in," he hollers.

I take a deep breath preparing myself for what I'm about to do. I've thought it over. More times than I care to admit. I even talked it out with the guys. For the most part, they all agreed with me. A few didn't, but who the fuck are they to decide what I do anyhow? I ignored their asses.

"Hey, Prez," I say when we walk in. Hawk stands in front of his desk with a stack of papers in front of him.

"Come on up here," he says waving his hand in the air at me. I pull Lyric up with me, standing in front of him.

"Now, you're sure this is what you want to do?" he asks looking me in the eyes. I nod my head, squeezing Lyric's hand tighter.

"Goddamn right," I tell him.

"What's going on?" Lyric asks looking between the two of us.

"His will. Crow wants everything he has to go to you in the event of his death," Hawk says solemnly.

Lyric instantly pulls her hand away from me. Her gaze is unfocused as she looks around the room. When she starts toward the door, I move quickly and grab her.

"Don't do this shit now, Crow! Why now?" she asks, her eyes slowly losing their glow.

"I need to know that it's in place. I'm not goin' to die today, Lyric, but I want this ready." She shakes her head before looking at Hawk.

"Tell him this is stupid! Tell him no!" she snaps. I look over my shoulder at Hawk but he just shrugs.

"Crow thinks it's for the best. I agree with him. When you live like we do, you never know when the end might come. He wants his shit in place, I can't blame him there." I grin at him. At least he has my back on this one.

"Fuck that! I'm not signing shit." Lyric crosses her arms over her chest and glares at me. Defiant. Yeah, that's her alright.

"Have you learned nothin' from that dressin' room?" I ask her mimicking her stance.

"What happened in the dressin' room?" Hawk asks with a chuckle, but neither of us answer him.

"Do this for me, Lyric. I need you to be taken care of. I need to know that I have this in place. I didn't say I was dyin' tomorrow, darlin'. Just please do this for me. I love you. You know that," I plead with her. Slowly her arms fall to her sides. She gives me a nasty look before walking past me and back to the desk. Grabbing a pen, she looks to Hawk. He points out where she needs to sign and I watch her with pride as she does it. Once she's done, she slams the pen onto the desk.

"Happy now?" she snaps at me. I nod my head, grab her arm and pull her into my chest.

"Thank you. It really settles somethin' in me to know that you will be taken care of. I love you," I whisper against her lips.

"I love you too, Crow. More than you know."

"Go get ready. Told you we're goin' out. I need to talk a few things over with Hawk." I kiss her quickly and give her a little push toward the door. She smiles at me but goes. Hearing the door click shut behind her, I blow out a breath.

"You sure about all this?" Hawk asks, his voice lowering. I know this is hard on everyone. We've been family for so long.

"It's right. It feels right. You know, I've spent so many years just tryin' to figure out where I needed to be." Shaking my head, I run my hand over my scalp. "Every year felt like the last, you know? I wanted it to be the last, but then somethin' kept me from doin' it every goddamn time. Then Lyric was sittin' in that fuckin' warehouse. She looked so hurt and pained. It fuckin' gutted me that there was someone else out there that felt even the tiniest bit of what I did. When I looked in her eyes, I lost it. The will just left my body."

"Does that mean you're rethinkin' it all? Maybe start the chemo?" Hawk asks.

"No. That's the thing, brother. She makes it all the more real. I miss Gabe, brother. I miss my son. So much that it kills me inside. Seein' her smile though, fuck! I want that for her. I want her to have whatever she's always dreamt of. My heart feels full and so does my life when I see her smile."

Hawk nods his head. "I get it. You might not think so, but I do. Just remember her, Crow. Let her be the one who takes you through each day. See where things go before you just check out. You deserve that much. I've known you since you were fuckin' ten, brother. You're like a son to me and losin' you is gonna hit me just as hard. You know that! Think about it, yeah? The paperwork is all in order, just think about it." Hawk walks around the table and pulls me into a hug.

"I will. I'll think about it, brother." Hawk pulls back and nods. I take that as my cue that we're done here. I turn on my heel and head out of his office. As I make my way down the hallway, I stop and look at the pictures hung on the wall. All the brothers who have died before me. Every one of them had a place here. They still do.

"I'm gonna be up there sooner than they all think," I grumble to myself. I take a deep breath and head out of the clubhouse ready to shower and get my night with Lyric started. As much as I love the club life, this life isn't entirely Lyric's. She's grown to love it here, she's told me time and time again, but she isn't your typical old lady. She's mine, that much is for damn sure, but this world

131

isn't hers. I want to take her out and show her just how much I love her. How much she means to me. I want her to have at least one normal night without club business or my health getting in the way of it.

Chapter 21

I showered quickly and got dressed. Lyric was in the bedroom getting dressed when I got back. I can't wait to spend a simple night out with her. She deserves so much more than me, but I want her to have a good time and will do anything to make that happen. I look at myself in the mirror and I barely recognize myself anymore. It isn't just the shaved head either. It's my whole being. Nothing seems normal about me anymore. My heart still beats, but I don't feel alive, not in the sense that I should.

"Crow?" A soft knock and her voice drifts through the room.

"Yeah. I'm comin'," I tell her. I blow out a breath and reach for the door knob. Turning it slowly, I pull it open and my heart leaps. Lyric stands there looking like a movie star. She's gorgeous. I've never seen anything like her. I gasp before I step into her space, wrapping my arms around her waist.

"You have to be the most beautiful person I've ever seen." I press a kiss to her neck, her body trembling in my grasp.

"You don't look so bad yourself," she whispers. I pull back and look her up and down. That purple dress was the best fucking choice I've ever made.

"You like it?" Lyric says before twirling around. My chest tightens. I can't imagine anything looking as good as she does right now.

"I like it so much I'm debatin' takin' you out. I might keep you all to myself." I groan as my dick hardens in my pants. Lyric giggles before kissing my cheek.

"Not a chance. You got me all dressed up and now I want to go. Where are we going anyway?" she asks. I grin and take her hand in mine, leading her down the hallway.

"Why are you askin' so many questions? I said I'm takin' you out. On a date." Even the words sound so foreign to me. I have never dated. Not since I was a kid, and even then, it wasn't a real date. Lyric tenses and stops right in front of the door.

"What is it?"

"I've never been on a date, Crow." If my heart could break any further, it just did. Hearing those words leave her mouth hurt me.

"If we're bein' honest, I've never dated either. I've always fucked and walked. I guess we are doin' all kinds of first things huh?" I ask her. Lyric's eyes find mine, a soft smile curling her lips. I lean down and capture them in the perfect kiss. When I pull away, she smiles at me.

"I guess we are. I don't know how to thank you, Crow. You do so much for me," she says. She doesn't know how much her words mean to me.

"Bein' with you calms me, Lyric. It makes everything feel like it's goin' to be okay. You're my stone. The rock that holds me down and centers me." Tears fill her blue eyes making me smile. Reaching up, I wipe them away with my thumbs.

"No cryin'. Remember? It's a good night." Lyric nods her head, straightening her spine.

As I lead her out to the truck, so many things weigh on me. The shit with the Ancients. Shit with myself. Leaving Lyric doesn't sit high on my priority list. I don't want to leave her. I don't want to let her down either, but there is a hollow spot inside of me that will never be filled unless I'm with my son. Despite that, being with Lyric heals a part of me. Holding her in my arms gives me something real. It gives me hope that there are brighter days out there and not just the dark loneliness that I've always felt. Maybe the guys were right. Maybe I should give this a chance with her. Who the hell knows? Maybe I will stick around a little longer than I planned to.

"Where'd you go?" Lyric asks as I open the door for her.

"I was just thinkin' about some shit the guys said," I tell her as I hold her hand, helping her into the truck. When she's settled in her seat, she grabs my face in her hands.

"What did they say?" she asks, her lips so close to mine.

"That I should stick around with you for a while. Think about my own plans, about who I might be hurtin'." Lyric smiles, pressing her lips against mine as if she could read my mind. It's like she knew I was rethinking it. Debating with myself.

"And you are going to, right?" she whispers against my lips. Shaking my head slightly, I wrap my hand around the back of her neck, keeping her close.

"I might just. That'd mean you'd be stuck with me a while. You think you can handle that?" I ask her. Lyric giggles and it's like music to my ears.

"I think I can. Well, I guess that depends on how this whole date goes tonight. I'm nervous," she says with a smile.

"Well, I plan on gettin' that goodnight kiss," I tease her. Lyric pulls away laughing.

"Just a kiss? Does that mean I get some sleep tonight?"

"When do I not let you sleep?" I ask pretending to be offended.

"Every night!" she squeals.

"Ok. I won't touch you then. I'll whisper dirty fuckin' words in your ear all night. About how I wanted to lick your pussy until you explode on my tongue. Or how I wanna pull your hair and fuck you until you come screamin'." Lyric's body shivers and I laugh, stepping back. I close the door and walk around to my side.

"I win," I say as I climb in and start up the truck.

Chapter 22

"I can't believe you did all of this," Lyric whispers as she looks around the beach. I had the prospects come out ahead of time and get things set up for me. I have to say the little fucks did a great job. The blanket is spread over the sand, the soft flicker of the candles in the moonlight. It's goddamn perfect.

"Why not? You deserve it all, Lyric. I just wish I could give you more." She gasps as I lead her to the blanket. I motion for her to sit before taking the spot next to her. Lyric beams with happiness. I watch as her hair blows slightly in the wind, pushing it into her face. Reaching over, I slowly brush it behind her ear.

"You're beautiful."

"So are you," she says softly.

"I wanted to take you out. I wanted to let you see what it's like to have someone care about you. I care, Lyric. Probably more than I should. You mean a lot to me. It all happened in such a short amount of time. You threw me off my game, but I love that about you. You force me to rethink everything." Being honest with her isn't a hard thing to do. She makes it easy. I think that's why I

138

fell for her so quickly. Lyric is one of those people that make you want to open up to them. They give you so much strength that they don't even realize they are doing it.

"You're pretty great yourself, Crow. You didn't look at my weight; you looked at me like a person. There aren't many guys out there that do that you know?"

I know it all too well. I've seen it all first hand and especially with her but I've also seen her grow into a strong woman.

"The thing is, not all people realize what they're missin' when they do that shit. They don't realize that there is somethin' fuckin' special inside here," I say as I place my hand on her heart. Tears slip down her cheeks, but I'm not done yet. "Your size means nothin' when your heart is as big as it is. You have more strength in you than you even know. Lyric, you've shown me another side of myself that I didn't even know was in there. All I wanna do is give you the world." A sob catches in her throat. Lyric climbs to her knees, scooting closer to me. Her arms wrap around my neck as she cries. I can only hope they are happy tears. Slipping my arms around her waist, I hold her against me.

"You have to know all that's true, baby," I whisper into her neck. Pressing a kiss to her soft skin, she pulls back, grabbing my face in her hands.

"You mean everything to me, Crow. From that first day in the warehouse. I always knew there was something different about you. There was more than anyone else could see. You were so sad but there was a spark in you. I saw it. I thought about you all that day. When I saw you in that diner, I didn't know what to feel. I didn't want you to go. I'm glad that you asked me to go for a ride with you. So much has changed in my life and it's all because of you. I always looked at myself as nothing. I was always told I was nothing, but you make me feel so damn special. I've never felt this way before."

God, she means everything to me. I kiss her roughly, not letting even a breath of air get between us. As I hold her tightly, enjoying the warmth of her, I find myself wondering if this is what real love feels like. If this is what God wants from everyone. A love like this couldn't come twice in a lifetime. At least not for me but for her? I think that once she gets herself to where she needs to be, she can find anything. She can do anything. Lyric has an old spirit that deserves so much more than she has.

"Ok. If we don't eat, I can't take you to the movie," I tell her, wiping my own eyes when I pull away from her. Lyric giggles and sits back on the blanket. I grab the basket that the prospects put out here and open it up. The laugh that escapes me has Lyric wondering. I can see the look in her eyes.

"What? What did they do?" she asks. I slide the basket over in front of her, watching as she peeks inside. Her laughter warms my heart.

"Are you serious? What did you tell them to do?"

"Told them to pack a nice dinner. Guess they didn't get what I meant." I chuckle as I pull the pizza out of the basket. Only those idiots could fuck that up.

"I'm sorry," I tell her as I pass her a slice. Lyric laughs.

"It's perfect, Crow! Don't be sorry. This is all so amazing," she says.

We sit in silence as we eat and drink the beers the guys packed. At least they got that part right. I'm at peace with everything right now. The soft breeze reminds me that I'm still alive and breathing. The stars that sparkle in the sky remind me that there is life out there somewhere. When we're finished, I clean up our mess and lie back on the blanket, pulling Lyric down with me.

"Are you nervous about your audition?" I ask her. She takes a deep breath and sighs.

"Not really. I've been practicing. It's never really been hard for me to sing. It's just singing in front of people that freaks me out. A lot of them look at my size and turn their heads." She quietly admits what's bothering her. I pull her closer into my side.

"Not when they hear what comes out of your mouth. It's fuckin' stunnin'. I've never heard anyone that can sing like you," I tell her honestly.

"Thanks. It's always been so calming, you know? Letting things out like that. Luther never liked it. He always said it reminded him of my mom."

"He ain't shit to you anymore. You know that right?" I ask needing to hear her say it. I need her to know who her family is and it isn't him.

"I know, because of you. Will you be at the audition? Please tell me you will go with me." She begs.

"You really think I'd miss that? You lost your fuckin' mind. Of course, I'm gonna be there."

I press my lips into her hair. Inhaling her scent, all I want to do is get inside of her. I want to fuck her until I'm all she can think about but now isn't the time.

"We need to go if we're gonna make the movie," I tell her. Lyric sighs like she's perfectly content lying here, but our night isn't over yet.

Chapter 23

The movie was good. I haven't been to one since I was younger. Lyric seemed to enjoy it too, but now she seems a little nervous. I can't say that I blame her at all because I'm just as nervous as she is.

"I know this seems strange. Fuck, it probably is downright stupid, but I feel like I need to do this." I tell her as we walk along the small path.

"It's not stupid, Crow. I'm honored that you brought me here," she says with a sniffle.

I know she's crying. I can hear her but I can't bring myself to look over for fear that I may join in. I can't let myself go like that until I finish what I came here to do. When we get to this headstone, I stop and look down at it. I had it made into the shape of a truck, just what he liked.

"He loved trucks. I always tried to get him into bikes, but Gabe was stubborn. He wanted what he wanted. He would always say he was gonna be a truck driver one day." I chuckle at the memory. Lyric's hand tightens around mine.

"Wonder where he got the stubborn streak from?" she teases.

"Yeah, he was like me a lot. He was always by my side. At first, I was scared shitless takin' care of a baby on my own. It was the strangest thing. He would cry all night long. I would walk around just holdin' him. The club girls would always try to get him and help out. Said he needed a woman's touch. I just shook them off. He just needed his daddy and a little love." I take a breath and push the tears that clog my throat back before I continue. "As he got older, he got easier. He was such an easy goin' kid. He went along with whatever I said to do. He never gave me trouble. He was the perfect kid. He was my kid. As he grew up though, he would ask about his momma. I would just tell him she wasn't ready. I never wanted him to know that she didn't want him, ya know? It was better to tell him she wasn't ready to be a mom yet. Even though I hated her fuckin' ass for walkin' away, I knew I couldn't say that to him. He was too young to understand all that. Sometimes I wished I would have told him." My head drops forward, my heart beating rapidly. It's been a while since I've been here and I've never brought anyone with me. I know the guys sometimes come out here, but I've always been alone.

"He loved his daddy. You know that, right?" Lyric asks me. I nod my head as a tear slips free. I

145

wipe it away before pulling my phone out of my pocket and scrolling through the pictures. I don't say anything, just pass her the phone.

"Crow! Oh my God, he looked just like you!" Lyric exclaims.

I laugh a little before looking over at the phone with her. Those big brown eyes that I loved to look at all the time. The smile on his face. He was the best thing that ever happened to me.

"He was all his daddy except for the bikes. He was a truck man. Never cared about the bike. He loved the clubhouse though. Used to get so fuckin' excited to go there. I think he liked all the commotion," I tell her. Lyric passes my phone back before wrapping her arm around my waist.

"Thank you for bringing me here. It means everything to me."

"I needed you to come. I needed you to know the other important part of my life, Lyric. You and him - that's all that's ever really mattered to me. I thought about pushin' you away. I thought that if I could stay my distance, nothin' would matter, but I couldn't. And you matter. More than I'd like to admit to myself most days. Gabe was a light in my life. He brought the good parts out of me and after he was killed, I lost it," I tell her.

"Did you ever find the guys that did it?" she asks softly, sounding unsure if she should ask.

"No. I looked. I searched. One day, I just gave up. I knew they were out there, but I didn't have it in me to look any longer. I just wanted to die. I'd drink myself into a deep sleep most of the time. I'd go out on the shit runs hopin' that God would finally give me the peace I wanted so much. He never did. And there were times I'd wonder why."

"Me," she says abruptly. "You're still here because of me. You were meant to cross my path. You're here to show me the way." She breaks into tears before I pull her into my chest. She realizes it just as much as I did.

"I believe that too. I didn't want to at first, but the more I was with you, the more I knew it. You're the reason I'm still here." Lyric pulls her head out of my chest. She looks up at me with her tear streaked face before kissing me. I hold onto her like she's my lifeline. After standing like this in each other's arms for what seems like hours, she pulls back. She turns toward Gabe's headstone and sits on the grass. She motions for me to follow her, which I do.

"When my mom died, I always believed she was out there somewhere. I didn't know where or how, but I had to believe that. You know he's out there, Crow. He was so young. He didn't deserve that, but you know what? He didn't have to face this world. He didn't have to feel any of the pain that the rest of us have. He's free. Free to do whatever he wants. Free to roam the heavens and watch over his daddy. He was lucky to have you." My heart nearly rips right out of my chest. How can she know that?

"I love you, Lyric." The only words that I can think slip from my lips. Lyric grabs my hand, squeezing it tightly.

"I love you, too."

Chapter 24

We ended our night at the cemetery after our date. I must say that is probably the best time I've ever had in my life as far as with a woman goes. My hearts felt content since then. As I sit in church watching the guys talk amongst themselves until Hawk comes in, I'm at ease. This whole situation has turned into more than I ever thought it would. I never imagined finding a woman or finding a woman that I could see a future with. Lyric kind of fell in my lap and I can't be sorry for that. She's shown me more about myself than anyone else ever has. She makes me rethink things and want to change. Although I can't say that I have completely changed my mind about my future, she has given me plenty to think about. When Hawk speaks, everyone goes silent. We all turn to face the man in charge.

"We know Ancients are still out there roamin' around. We got a run tonight though. Fucked up thing is we are runnin' right through their turf. I don't like it, but there is no way around it. Farmer has a lot of money ridin' on us movin' this product for him. We have a lot ridin' on it too. Smokey has a meetin' with Henley about how shit with Ancients is gonna go down. That means I need Crow, Draven, and Ruger on this one. Obviously I'll be throwin' some other guys in, but you three need to be on lead. I don't want no shit comin' down while we're short on guys and I need my best up front." Farmer isn't my favorite person but we do move a lot of drugs for him.

The guys grunt as I nod my head. I'm ready for a run. We haven't been on one in a while and that's starting to take a toll on me too. I live for this life. I love everything about it. Even when shit gets nasty and bloody.

"We heard anything about them knowin' we're runnin' through there?" I ask wondering.

"Not yet. Wouldn't surprise me if they didn't know at all. They aren't the smartest motherfuckers out there. They did try to get up with those little street riders." Hawk chuckles. The rest of us follow along. He has a good point. If they were that easy to get to, they weren't the best group to choose.

"Anything else?" Hawk asks looking around the table.

Everyone shakes their heads before he slams the gavel down. The guys slowly rise and filter out but I linger. I don't know why I sit here. Maybe the feeling of being at this table brings me some kind of relief. I don't really know anymore.

"How'd she handle the surprise?" Hawk asks, sitting in the chair next to me. I pull out my pack of cigarettes and light one up.

"Surprisingly well. She always amazes me though," I say as I blow the smoke through my nose.

"And Gabe?" Just hearing his name slices through my heart. I miss his so much it physically hurts.

"Better than I thought. She listened. We talked." I shrug. We sit in silence for a long time, just letting things linger in the air. Hawk has always been a man of many words so it's strange to sit here in silence with him. I'm about to stand up when he speaks.

"You know, I give you a lot of hell for your decisions every year. You walk out those doors and a piece of me goes with you, Crow. Every fuckin' year I watch you spiral out of control and I wonder if this is gonna be the last time I see you. It rips us all apart. It took everything we had to hold Ruger back this year. I don't know how he's gonna take shit if it comes. Now I'm not tellin' you to go all fuckin' girly on his ass but I think some kind of talk might do him good."

Just hearing him say that to me makes my heart hurt worse. Ruger has been one of my best friends since I was a kid. He's always been by my side and the thought of hurting him doesn't sit well with me.

"I know, brother. I don't wanna hurt anyone, it's not what that's about. It's about my heart not bein' whole anymore. It's about the fuckin' ache in my chest. That time of year rolls around and I can feel myself slowly dyin', yeah? It's hard to handle."

Hawk nods knowing all too well what pain feels like. He slaps a hand on my shoulder and says, "I know. More than you think, I know. Go see your girl before you head out."

I nod my head and shove out of the chair and head out into the hallway. As I step into the main room I grin over at Ruger and Kira. I swear that girl was made for him. Regardless of what she's been through, she still found it in herself to love that beast of a man. Ruger catches me looking and lifts his chin. I do it right back before heading out the side door. As soon as I step out, she's there. Just like always, she's there.

"Where do you think you're goin'?" I ask her with a grin. She smiles up at me with that perfect smile that could melt hearts. Hell, it has mine.

"Looking for you. Sherry wants to go hang out for a while. I told her I would since I haven't seen her in so long." Wrapping my arms around her waist, I peer down at her.

"Yeah? What's the plan? Strippers?" I wiggle my eyebrows at her.

"If I want a show, I'll ask you. I don't really know what she wants to do," she says. My heart pounds in my chest. This woman.

"Have fun. You deserve it."

"What are you going to do without me?" she teases with a smile.

"I was just comin' to find you. I got a run tonight. Probably be back late." I lean down and press my lips to hers. Since we've found out about the cancer, Lyric worries when I ride. She doesn't say anything but I can feel it when she tenses up. I can't say that I blame her either. I do get tired as hell but I push through it. I have no other choice and this is my life. I told Hawk that I didn't want to be treated any differently after we found out and he hasn't. That much I'm grateful for.

"Sleep in tomorrow?" she asks, pressing her lips to my neck. Shit, if she keeps doing that I may just change my mind.

"If you plan on kissin' me like that, we might need a few days." Lyric giggles and my heart soars.

"Deal."

"Good. Make sure you text me and let me know you're good. I can send a prospect if you want," I offer. I know she will say no, she always does. Lyric isn't in any kind of danger but I still make the offer so that she feels safe.

"No. I think we can handle it. Besides, I don't plan on staying out all night. I want to be here when you get back." Fuck this girl is so damn perfect.

"Naked?"

"Crow."

"Lyric."

"Fine. Naked."

"Knew I'd win."

Chapter 25

"You afraid to die?" Ruger asks as we lean against the van that's being loaded. The ride down here went smooth but that means shit for the ride back.

"No. It seems easy enough." I chuckle. The silence lingers. Ruger lost in his own thoughts. I've thought about death a lot. Not just after I found out about the cancer but before. I always knew it was inevitable. It's always a risk we take. It's always out there lurking. Never having much to live for after Gabe has really set me up for it. I accept it and when it's time, I will gladly go down.

"You ever wonder what hell's gonna be like?" I turn my head and glare at him thinking he's joking but he isn't. His face is stone.

"Who says we're goin' to hell?" I joke lightly. Ruger chuckles.

"Don't think heaven would want us bastards."

"Don't know, brother. Maybe there isn't either one. Maybe it's just all peaceful and shit. We can all be together with no fuckin' wars and no beefs. Fuck if I know, man." I grab a cigarette and light it up as Ruger nods his head.

"Wouldn't that be some shit? All of us in the calm. That's not somethin' I've ever seen or felt before." He chuckles. I have to agree. Our lives may be calm at times but in the line of work we do, there is always something around every corner.

"You scared of it, brother?" I ask him intrigued now.

"I ain't scared of much, man, but dyin'? Fuck! I'm scared shitless. It's permanent. It can't be taken back and you have no fuckin' clue where you're goin'. Plus, after all the shit I've done? I don't even want to think about what will happen to me after this world." Ruger shoves off the truck and walks around to the back, checking the loading progress. I let his words hang in the air as I smoke.

"Long day?" Draven walks over, stopping in front of me.

"Not bad. Ready to get home and get some pussy," I tell him. Draven laughs and slaps a hand on my shoulder.

"Keep your eyes open on the way back. Not sure where these motherfuckers are. Not even Mystic got a hit on them."

His words turn my stomach. If Mystic couldn't find them, no one can. I flick my cigarette to the ground and crush it under my boot before following Draven around to the back of the truck.

"Fuck, that's one big ass load." I whistle as I look in the back. It's damn near full.

"Sure as hell is. Wonder what kind of party he's havin'." Draven chuckles. I nod before closing one of the doors. Ruger slams the other door before one of Farmer's guys throws a lock on it.

"Farmer said to let you know that if that lock comes off, so does your head," he growls in my direction. I take a step closer to him, my fist balled at my side. We may run shit for Farmer, but he isn't one to threaten people.

"That so? Warn me one more time and you can pick your teeth up and hand them to him," I growl in return. Ruger laughs behind me, knowing damn good and well I want a fight. I think I've kind of been trying to pick one with people for a while now, just not one of my boys.

"Fuck you, man. You think I'm scared of you?" The man bows up at me.

I cock my head to the side and look at him. Making sure he really knows what he's about to step into before I unleash. All the pent-up energy. All the stress, pain, and anger explode through my fists. I pound the hell out of him, blow after blow. He gets some swings in before he's on top of me.

"Piece of shit!" he roars, his right fist slamming into my jaw. I can feel my teeth clatter together and I taste blood in my mouth. He throws a few more before I dodge them and flip his ass off me. I climb to my feet, watching the little prick. Turning my head to the side, I spit the blood from my mouth.

"I got your piece of shit right here," I say pointing at him. He moves back in at me and I slam a fist into his ribs. It feels good to have some kind of energy. Feels damn good. Once the fucker falls on his ass, I start to move back in, but Ruger grabs my shoulder, halting me.

"We need to ride, brother. Fuck him." Ruger spits on the asshole lying on the ground. I reach up, wiping the blood from my face. I have to say I feel pumped up and energized. I haven't felt this alive in a long time. My muscles are tight and ready for more but I know we need to head out.

"Fuckin' prick. Come see me when you grow some balls, you fuckin' pussy." I spit more blood from my mouth onto the ground as Ruger throws his arm over my shoulder and leads me toward the bikes in a laughing fit.

"You had to do it, didn't you? I could feel the fuckin' tension rollin' off you, man. I waited to see if you'd do it. Hell, I almost pushed that pussy into you just to see you hit him." Ruger laughs hysterically. I shake my head and reach up, wiping the blood from my eye so that I can see.

"You're fuckin' insane." I laugh along with him.

"Goddamn right I am. You ain't far behind, motherfucker. I bet you would have killed him if I would have let it keep goin'." The asshole laughs harder. I don't see why this is funny but I go with it.

"You're probably right." I grab my helmet and slide it on my head. In fact, I know he's right. I wanted to feel something, anything so goddamn bad.

Chapter 26

We made it through Ancients' turf with no problems. That alone doesn't sit well with me. They should have been on us but they weren't. It makes me uneasy. Where the hell are they? What are they up to? Ruger, me, and about six more guys follow closely behind the truck as Draven took some guys and went up front. This isn't our typical riding style either. Usually we're a few blocks to a few miles behind our product, but with as many drugs that are rolling around in the back of that truck, we had to play it closer. It doesn't bother me but it does set me on edge. When there are too many guys too close, it draws attention from not only rival clubs but the cops. Lately our run with the cops hasn't been the best and that makes me nervous.

So far the ride has been silent as I let the feeling of kicking that fucker's ass race through my system. I know when I come down, I'm going to hit rock bottom. Hard. I can feel the effects. I don't like it but this damn cancer wears me down. Some people would stop living and jump at the chance to have the chemo but not me. I don't want that poison in my body. As my mind wanders, shots spray past us, lodging into the back of the truck. I jerk my eyes to Ruger's hoping like hell he saw that shit too. He nods his head once as I check my mirrors. Fuck! Just when we were almost in the clear.

Ruger's on his cell, managing his bike with one hand. He makes the calls that set a plan into action. We all know the plan. We've been over it a million times, and in some cases, we've executed it perfectly. I can only hope this time is one of those perfectly executed. With seconds to spare, we speed up. I watch my mirrors as adrenaline races through my body. Reaching around, I grab my gun before positioning it between my legs. Now that I'm ready to fire, I nod over at Ruger. The guys behind us damn well better be paying attention or they are in our line of fire. The truck speeds up, taking off from view as we spin our bikes around on a dime. The wind whipping around me gives me an even bigger thrill. We climb off quickly, and hold our guns out, ready to fire. As soon as we see the motherfuckers round the corner, it's game time.

"Here we go!" Ruger roars like a fucking lion. He walks forward, firing shot after shot as his crazy ass walks toward them. I fire as do the other guys. Bodies begin to fall, bikes skidding to a halt. Laughter erupts out of me as a few of them haul ass to turn around and run. Fucking cowards. Once there are no Ancients left in sight moving, I shove my gun into the back of my jeans and walk toward them. Ruger isn't far behind me as he calls to let Draven know we're all good here.

"Fuckin' pricks," I mumble as I kick a booted foot in front of me. Movement catches my eye and I quickly pull my gun, aiming at the sight.

"You better think real hard before makin' another move," I warn, my tone deadly. The movement slowly comes out of the brush on the side of the road and my heart drops along with my gun.

"Who the fuck are you?" I ask when I see the girl standing there looking scared to death. Ruger walks up next to me and grunts.

"Fuck," he mumbles.

"I'm nobody. I'm sorry. I wasn't... I shouldn't." She can't even speak. She's so worked up she can't form a sentence.

"You ain't a nobody. You just watched us kill them." I motion to the dead bodies with my gun. The girl watches me intently but doesn't move aside from the shaking in her limbs.

"I didn't see anything!" she yells quickly. Ruger chuckles before he walks over to her, stepping into her space.

"You didn't see nothin'? Like nothin' at all?" he asks, wrapping his hand around the back of her neck. He holds tightly as her body trembles.

"No. I didn't see anything. I promise!" she cries. I shake my head not knowing what to do here. We don't typically leave any kind of witnesses but this is just a girl.

"How old are you?" I ask, moving closer as I stuff my gun into the back of my jeans once more.

"Don't do this, Crow," Ruger all but whines. I just chuckle.

"How old?" I ask again when she doesn't answer me.

"Seventeen," she says quickly. I drag my gaze to Ruger's. I can see the way he's seething already.

"Fuck, man! She's on you!" he snaps, shoving the girl into my arms. She stumbles, but I catch her before she can fall. Her body is shuddering from fear. An all too familiar memory flashes behind my eyes. His face. The way he looked at me. The way his body shook. I can't breathe. I can't make my body work. I'm numb and all I can do is gasp for air.

"Hey! There's something wrong with him!" I can hear the girl yelling but I can't see. It's as if the world is slowly opening up around me and sucking me into its depths.

"Crow!" Ruger roars before I can feel him next to me. "Take deep breaths, brother," he says, trying to bring me back.

I slowly inhale through my nose trying to calm the storm that has whirled its way into my body, into my mind. Slowly, I take as many breaths as I can before things start to slow down. The world slowly comes back into view. When I can focus, I see the girl leaning over me, worry etched across her face.

"Are you okay?" she asks quickly. I nod my head once and shove myself up to a sitting position.

"Fuck," I grumble.

"Yo, Ruger! Hawk wants us back at the clubhouse now!" Another of the guys hollers from next to us.

"Can you ride?" Ruger looks me in the eye. I nod my head before he grabs my arm, pulling me up. The girl stands to the side looking as worried as ever. She's probably thinking we are just going to leave her to the mess we made. Sirens ring in the distance, and that's all I need to get my ass in gear. Shaking my head, I grab the girl's wrist and pull her along with me toward my bike.

"Are you sure you're okay to drive? What are you going to do to me?" Her voice breaks as my head swims. I can't handle this right now. I feel like shit and now I'm stuck with this girl I don't even know.

"I'm fine. Get the fuck on the bike," I growl. My mood has shifted to a shitty one. I don't mean to take it out on her, but she's not in a position to question me right now. I shove my helmet into her hands and climb on my bike waiting on her. She hurriedly slides the helmet on before climbing on behind me. I don't take a last look around, I know there are cops coming. I rev up my bike and take off right behind the rest of the guys.

The rest of the ride to the clubhouse is tense. I don't know what Hawk is going to do with this girl now that she's witnessed us killing a bunch of rivals. I don't know how far he will go with her, and for some goddamn reason that bothers me to even think about it. Her hands shake as she holds onto me. I can't blame her. She just witnessed something no other seventeen-year-old kid should have to. Most of the guys are ruthless and that includes when it comes to women. They don't care what happens to them, they just want things their way. I'm not one of them. I'm the odd one out. I don't go after women unless it's a huge necessity.

Pulling into the compound, my heart stammers in my chest. Something about this girl that's hanging onto me for dear life reminded me of Gabe. The fear I saw in her was the same fear I saw in him, and I don't think I can let go of that. I don't think Ruger will be getting this one in the dungeon unless he goes through my dead body first.

Chapter 27

I spot Hawk and Smokey standing right outside the garage as we pull in. The truck is being taken underground until all this gets sorted out. I watch as the garage door closes, the truck disappearing from view. Pulling into my spot, I cut the engine and climb off. The girl climbs off behind me, passing me my helmet.

"Heard you had an issue," Hawk says walking toward us. His eyes are on her and they look deadly.

"Not so much," I say grabbing the pack of cigarettes from my pocket and lighting one up. I turn to my left and offer the girl one but she shakes her head no. I shrug and turn back to Hawk.

"What's that then?" He nods to the girl that now feels like she's clinging to me for dear life. Her body is so close to mine that I can feel every involuntary shudder.

"A kid," I tell him blowing out a ring of smoke. Hawk watches me for a long minute before moving closer.

"Who the hell are you and where did you come from? What the fuck were you doin' out there?" he snaps. The girl literally jumps, her fingers coiling into the back of my cut.

"It's okay, darlin'. Answer his questions," I tell her, wrapping an arm around her shoulder and pulling her up next to me.

"I had nowhere else to go. I thought you were my foster dad. He…" Her words trail off ripping me in half. I don't need her to finish what she's saying.

"How old are you?" Hawk asks, his eyes narrowed at her.

"Seventeen."

"That's legal age to move out, darlin'. What the hell were you stayin' there for if he hurt you?" Hawk asks. Annoyance laces his voice, but I keep a firm grip on the girl.

"I had nowhere else to go. I didn't see anything. I won't say anything, I promise," she sobs.

Hawk runs his hand through his hair before he says, "Well which is? You didn't see or you won't tell?" he roars. My muscles coil tighter. I don't want to fight my own prez, but he's pushing his luck with me right now. She's a kid.

"Both!" she yells.

"She's a kid, Hawk," I say, my voice a little lower than I meant it to be.

"She's a witness, Crow." He shakes his head.

"Maybe, but she's a fuckin' kid," I growl. Hawk paces in front of us a minute before he glances to Smokey. He gives him a quick nod before dragging his gaze to me.

"Take her home with you for tonight. Get her settled. Church in the mornin'. Bring her with," Smokey says.

I blow out another ring of smoke before pulling the girl along with me. I opt to walk over to the house instead of driving the bike, giving me a chance to question her.

"What's your name?" I ask.

"Wendy."

"Well, Wendy. You are stuck in a very fucked-up situation right now. We don't leave witnesses," I tell her. She starts to sob again and it kills me.

"I didn't say I was gonna kill you. I just need to know a little more about you. You ever seen one of these clubs before?"

She shakes her head quickly. "I was trying to get away from him is all. I heard the bikes and thought he was looking for me. I hid in the brush so I could see when he was gone. I was just going to run and never stop." She cries harder. My chest tightens as we make our way to the house. I see Lyric's car in the driveway and my heart leaps.

"Here's the thing. You're gonna have to explain yourself to everyone tomorrow, not just me. They will decide what they wanna do with you, but I won't let them hurt you, got it? You're a kid. I wouldn't let them do shit unless they kill me first. Kids aren't my style. Now, this is my place. This compound is surrounded as you saw when we came in. There is no way out. Don't give them a reason to not trust your word. I'll do what I can." She nods her head as we walk up onto the porch. When I shove the door open, she steps inside with me right behind her. Lyric stands there dumbfounded.

"Hey, baby," I say as I walk toward her. Pulling her into my arms, I kiss her roughly with everything I have in me. When I pull back, Lyric gasps.

"What happened to you?" Her hands come up to my face. Her fingers tremble as they trail over the cuts and bruises.

"A little fight. I'm fine. Hey, baby, this is Wendy. She's stayin' here tonight. You think you can talk to her, get her squared away for the night in the spare room?" She must be able to see the pleading in my eyes. She smiles and kisses me again before walking past me.

I hear her talk to Wendy as I make my way down the hallway. Heading straight into the bathroom, I turn the water on the hottest I can stand it before climbing in. I need to burn away this night. I need it to disappear from my mind if only for a few minutes. Standing under the hot stream of water, I sigh. The visions that assaulted me tonight were more vivid than they have ever been. Looking into the big brown eyes of Wendy, I saw Gabe. I don't know what to make of it. I don't know how I should feel but I wash quickly and climb out of the shower. Drying off in record time, I wrap the towel around my waist and head into the hallway. The spare room door is closed and soft sobs come from inside. It breaks my heart that Wendy has been placed in this shitty situation for no other reason than trying to escape her past. When I open the door to the bedroom, Lyric is lying there. She turns her head to look at me and tears form in my eyes.

"Crow." She says my name softly. I walk over and grab my shorts, tossing the towel, and sliding them on. Climbing on the bed, I lie down and snuggle up against her. I just need to hold her. To be close to her.

"Her foster dad abused her. She has marks all over her body. She's scared to death," Lyric says as I hold her head to my chest.

"I won't let the guys do anything stupid. I just need to hold you right now, yeah?" Lyric sobs into my chest. I know this has to be killing her to see another girl just like her. I hold her tighter than I ever have and let my own tears fall free.

"And you?"

"I saw Gabe in her eyes. My world spun out of control and I lost it a minute. I'm back now," I say not truly sounding like myself.

"Are you?"

"I don't know, Lyric. I don't know, baby."

Chapter 28

I opted out of the meeting on Wendy. I told them my piece on it and left. Ruger agreed with me that she wouldn't be hurt. I don't know if they are letting her go or keeping her, but she won't be harmed. My day's is to focus on Lyric. Today is her big audition. She's nervous as hell, which makes her look sexy as fuck. Her cheeks are pink and she paces around mumbling to herself. It makes me smile.

"Stop, Crow. I mean it. That cocky ass grin isn't helping at all," she says with a nasty look on her face but in her eyes, she's loving me.

"I can be cocky. My baby is about to kill that shit out there." I nod toward the stage.

"What if I don't?" she asks, her nervous fucking with her head.

"You will. Don't doubt yourself, darlin'." I wink at her when the woman comes around the curtain to get her. Lyric freezes. I move quickly to her side, pulling her into my arms.

"It's me, Lyric. You're only singin' to me. No one else out there matters. None of them. You hear me? Look for me," I whisper in her ear. She nods her head and I press a kiss to her cheek. I haul ass out into the small audience and stand right in the back. Right in the line of view.

Lyric walks onto the stage with a microphone in her hand when the music starts to play. As soon as she opens her mouth, the biggest smile I've ever had crosses my face. Her eyes find mine and the words just flow out of her. She's in the light - this is where she belongs. I don't give a shit what people think about her size, it's all her heart. That's what makes her beautiful. The way she can take all the pain of her past and force it out of herself through a song. She's mesmerizing. I'm transfixed on her. I can't hear anything else but her. When the song finishes, I roar with applause.

"You killed it! You fuckin' killed it, baby!" I don't give a shit about these pricks judging her. In my eyes, she's all that matters. Lyric smiles as a blush creeps up her cheeks.

I walk the aisle still clapping until I reach the stage. I hold my arms out to her, and when she lets me lift her down, I almost cry. She's never let me do this before.

"You were amazin'. I've never seen anything like it, Lyric," I whisper in her ear.

"I have to agree with your boyfriend. You were amazing. I'd like to offer you a spot in the show." A man's voice booms behind us. I pull away and spin us both. The man stands there in his overpriced suit smiling like a fool. I shove Lyric toward him. He extends his hand and she almost goes in for a hug. I can see her. She's so fucking happy right now. This is the Lyric I want to always remember.

"Thank you so much!" she says excitedly.

"The pleasure is mine." The man smiles back.

When Lyric turns to face me, I melt. The happiness that flows out of her is astounding. She leaps into my arms and I hold her tightly.

"Let's go. We got some celebratin' to do!" I tell her. Lyric laughs. I pull back and grab her hand. I can't wait to get her out of here and back home. I don't even make it that far. As soon as I see a side door, I'm yanking her into it.

"What are you doing?" she asks breathlessly.

I slowly unbutton my jeans and slide them down my legs. "Lift that dress beautiful and turn around." Lyric hesitates only for a second. She turns around and hikes up her dress.

"Goddamn. You didn't put panties on?" I ask as I move toward her. I run my hands over her ass, giving it a little slap. Lyric gasps before I grab her ass and position her the way I want her.

"We're going to get caught," she says breathlessly.

"Fuck them. I need you," I tell her. Shoving into her, she calls my name. It's the best sound I've ever heard. Gripping her hips, I slam into her. Thrust after thrust, I take what I want from her, what I need. The feeling of her wrapped around is perfect. It's a feeling I never want to let go. That thought alone scares the shit out of me.

"Come on, Lyric. You don't wanna get caught," I groan as I thrust harder. Her pussy clenches around me and my mind overloads. I explode inside of her at the same time she comes undone. Her body shudders as I catch my breath. Pulling out of her, I pull my jeans back up before adjusting her dress to cover her ass.

"I think I like getting fucked in the back room," Lyric giggles. I grab her and pull her to me, wrapping my hand around the back of her neck.

"Do you know how proud I am? That you got up there and let your emotions go?" I ask her seriously.

"I would have never been able to do it without you, Crow. You are everything. You are the one that makes me believe in myself," she says. Shaking my head, I rest my forehead against hers.

"You did it, Lyric. All I did was show you you could. This is all on you baby." The shine in her eyes is undeniable. So is the pain in my chest. This is the hardest thing I've ever had to do. Being torn between living and dying. What kind of people have to make that decision? I'm lost in her eyes. I'm lost in her. Lyric has my heart, she has to know that. She holds everything about me in her hands. I never want her to give it back either. Not now, not ever.

Chapter 29

I led Lyric into the clubhouse as soon as we got back. The thought of taking her home and fucking the hell out of her crossed my mind, but I knew everyone was waiting on her. They all knew it was audition day and Hawk wanted to make a big deal out of it. It makes me happy that they all want to play as big a role in this as they do. This club may be a lot of things, but when you get to the heart of it, we are some good bastards. Lyric's hand shakes as I let her go and walk away. All eyes are on her now.

"So, I made it!" Lyric says before the room goes up in screams. The girls all rush to her, hugging and congratulating her. Her smile couldn't possibly get any bigger. She shines the brightest in the room. I lean against the wall and watch her. She deserves this.

"Heard Henley caught up with the rest of those Ancients," Hawk says pulling my attention from Lyric to him.

"Yeah? Thank fuck. Cops didn't have shit on us?" I ask. That part has been making me nervous. Hawk shakes his head.

"Draven had James check shit out. Nothin' pointed this way. I think we're in the clear."

I nod my head and say a little thank you to myself that the we won't have any blow back from that. It's always a worry as it should be. When we do something of that magnitude, it typically causes a blow back that we never see coming.

"She's happy. I'm proud of her." Hawk nods toward Lyric.

"I'm damn proud of her. You should have seen her. She stood up there, her head held high. She just let it all go. Everything she had in her came out. I've never seen anything like it, Hawk. She takes my fuckin' breath away every time her mouth opens." Hawk watches me but I know he can sense my unease. He's always been able to.

"But?" he says.

"But this isn't my life to live. It's hers. This is her dream."

"Come on, Crow!" he snaps angrily.

Shrugging my shoulders, I sigh and take a drink of my beer. It is what it is. There is no changing facts. This is real life and this is who I am.

"I didn't think you'd change your mind. I kind of knew you wouldn't. In a way, I've been preparin' for the worst. I hate it, son. I fuckin' hate it and you know it but I also understand. I respect you way too much to not." His words bring a tear to my eye. "You were never like us. You were never a pissed at the world, ready to fuck anything with legs kind of guy. Gabe would be proud of you. I know he is. You give my grandson a hug for me when you see him, yeah?"

Slowly tears slide down my cheeks. I turn around and wipe them away as Hawk walks in the opposite direction. I saw the tears in his too. He may be right in a way. He's always known what was to come one day. Truth is, I'd fit better up north than I do here. I never liked hurting women. The guys here, although my brothers and best friends, they don't have hearts like mine. They're different. They can handle things that I never could, but that didn't stop them from taking me in and making me the man I am today.

Sometimes I dream that my life was different. I wonder what it would have been like if I wasn't a part of this club or if I had never had Gabe. The thought of not knowing him, even if for that little time, kills me. It won't settle inside of me. There are times I regret not finding the bastard who took him from me. There are times I regret not dying that night with him. Why did God decide to spare my life? Why did he want me to go on without the one thing that meant the world to me? None of it ever makes sense. At least, not until Lyric. I wholeheartedly believe that she is the reason that I'm still here and breathing. She's the purpose that I had to fulfill before I leave this earth, and I can't thank God enough for letting me have that time with her. She's become more than I ever dreamt she'd be. She holds my hand when I need it. She kisses away the tears when I cry. She's shown me a part of myself that no one else could have seen because I wasn't willing to let them. Lyric took that part. She took it the day she smiled at me in that diner.

"Hey." I hear a small voice behind me. I turn and look down at Wendy with a smile on her face.

"Hey. Doin' okay?" I ask. She watches me, no doubt seeing the tears for a second before she nods. I'm glad when she doesn't comment; I don't think I could explain this to her.

"I just wanted to say thank you. I mean for everything. Hawk said I could stick around and save up some money or he would put me on a bus to anywhere." She's so young. I hope she makes the right choice.

"What is it you're gonna do?"

"I'm going to stay. I mean, if that's alright with you. Hawk said I could move in with some of the girls so I'm not taking over your house, but I like Lyric. She understands me."

I nod my head before she throws her arms around my waist. Throwing mine around her, I hold her close. She isn't much different than Lyric. I have no doubt in my mind that these two are going to click. Lyric will become one of her biggest influences, I just know it. That's the kind of person that Lyric is.

"You can stay as long as you want. In fact, I'd like it if you'd stay with Lyric. I'm gonna have to leave soon and I think she could use the company." Wendy pulls back and looks up at me. This time I don't see Gabe. This time nothing flashes behind my eyes. Wendy nods her head quickly, a small smile on her face.

"Thank you," she whispers. I nod my head and watch her walk away and wonder if she was put in my path too. Was she meant to be in my life and I didn't know it? Was she here to help Lyric when I'm gone? So many unanswered question dance around in this head of mine. Lyric had said once before that I was meant to cross her path.

Maybe this is just another one of those times in our lives.

"You know what? I'm sick of women!" Smokey stomps up next to me. I can't help but laugh.

"Why is that?"

"Fuckin' Bray, brother. She wants another kid! I'm pretty sure I'm already fuckin' up my daughter's life. I don't need to do that to another one."

I laugh and take a long pull from my beer. "You ain't fuckin' her up. She's good, man. I see that bitin' shit is still the same." I chuckle as I look at the marks on Bray's neck.

"Some things can't change. I can't control myself, which is why I don't want another kid. I don't think I can handle I," Smokey admits before taking a long pull of his own beer.

"I get it. Just talk to her, brother." Smokey nods and leans against the wall next to me. I close my eyes as I think about tomorrow. Fuck. I need to get Lyric and get out of here. I need to have that time with her. I need to let her feel me and hear my heart.

Chapter 30

"We need to talk," I tell her as I pull her body back into mine. She looks over her should and grins at me.

"Then let's go home."

I nod my head and grab her hand. With our fingers intertwined, I lead her out the door and into the calm night.

"What do you want to talk about?"

"You know when I met you, I didn't think that you'd change me the way you have. I thought I would fuck you in the warehouse and walk. Or die. When I saw that you had taken the time to cover me up, I thought that maybe there was a reason that I didn't do it. A reason that I was still alive. Seein' you in that diner, I knew there was somethin' with you, but I wasn't sure what. I wanted to find out." I take a deep breath before I continue, knowing that I'm going to tear her apart. "The idea to try was always there. You have to know that it was nothin' against you, Lyric. You're perfect, and one day, a man will come along and love you like I do, maybe more. You'll move on and become somethin' that only others could dream to be. You have so much love to give and with me, you're wasitin' it. All of what you have in your heart deserves to be heard by everyone." Tears slide down Lyric's cheeks as I turn to face her.

"I don't want to know when, Crow. I don't think I could handle that. You can't tell me. Promise me," she begs. Sighing, I pull her head against my chest and kiss the top of her head. She's so fucking strong. One of the strongest people I know.

"I promise, but I want you to promise me somethin', too. Promise that you will move on. That you will go on and be who you were meant to be." A sob chokes me but I need to hear her say it. I need to know that my time here wasn't wasted.

"Crow. Fuck. You know how much you mean to me? How the hell do I move on from you? How?" She cries harder but I know she can do it. She has to. In this life there is no other choice. She will move on and become something that I already know I will be proud of.

"You're strong and you have a home. This is your home. Never doubt that and always come back, do you hear me? I don't want you anywhere near your stepdad ever again. And Wendy. Shit. You got your hands full with that one." Lyric giggles into my shirt. When she pulls back I can see the tears staining her cheeks.

"I promise, Crow."

That's all I needed.

"Now come on. I need to get inside of you before our adopted daughter comes home." Lyric laughs and grabs my hand in hers. As we walk back to the house, the world seems at ease. I feel it. This sense of peace isn't one that I've felt in a very long time.

"Tomorrow can we go get a tattoo?" she asks a little excitedly. I raise an eyebrow and she laughs.

"You want a tattoo? Of what?" She shrugs her shoulders making me laugh. I never knew she wanted a tattoo. Hell, if I did, I would have taken her a long time ago.

"You want to get inked but don't know what you want? Seems like a good plan!" I tease her.

"Shut up! I mean it. I really want one but I don't want to tell you what it is. I want it to be a surprise." Her eyes glisten with unshed tears. I reach up and brush them away from her cheeks.

"You want it, you got it. You know I'd give you anything, Lyric." She smiles but it doesn't meet her eyes. I'd give her anything except my life. That's the one thing I can't offer her and what I know she wants most.

We walk in silence back to the house. As soon as I have her in the house, I have her naked on her knees, not even making past the living room. I want to spend my night worshipping her body. I want her to remember just how fucking beautiful she truly is. Of all the women I've been with, Lyric is the best. She's always been different but that's what makes her special.

"Damn you look so good like this," I groan as I slide into her from behind. Lyric's pussy clenches around me and my mind spins.

"Don't go easy on me," Lyric purrs.

"Fuck, Lyric. I like when you talk like that." Gripping her hips, I thrust harder. I take her to a whole new level of pleasure. I push her limits and make her come over and over again.

When we're both fully satisfied, I hold her in my arms lying on the floor. I run my fingers through her hair. I keep my little piece of heaven in my arms until we both fall asleep.

Chapter 31

"Are you sure about this?" I ask her while we walk hand in hand.

"Yes! I've never been so sure." She grins. I nod my head and keep walking. Stopping in front of the tattoo shop, she looks a little nervous.

"You sure you don't want me to stay?"

Lyric shakes her head quickly. "No! I'll chicken out if you're here, and I told you I want it to be a surprise."

God, that smile. I want to savor it. I want to bottle up her happiness and keep it forever.

"I'm always with you, Lyric." I press my lips to hers. Lyric pulls me closer, kissing me harder. When I finally pull back, she smirks up at me.

"I know you are, Crow. I love you."

"I love you, baby."

"Ok. I'm going in," she says taking a deep breath.

I watch her hold her head high before walking into the shop. I shake my head and smile. She never stops amazing me. I watch through the window for a few minutes, letting the sight of her work its way through me. Lyric glances over her shoulder, blowing me a kiss that settles in my chest. I do the same back and watch as the artist leads her into the back.

Turning on my heel, I walk over a few blocks to the abandoned warehouse we met in. I climb the stairs and sit in the same spot. Was it always God's plan for me to meet her or did I stumble into it? Doesn't matter now. She's happy. She's alive and full of light.

So many things in life don't make sense. So many do. The thought that I have helped Lyric move forward in her life makes me feel like I've accomplished something good in my life. After Gabe died, I didn't see myself moving on. The world seemed to stop and I was stuck in the middle of all that darkness. Lyric was the light. She was the reason I was left on this earth so many times. She was the reason God wouldn't let me go. At first, I thought it was the devil holding me here, taunting me, but the more I thought it over the more I realized that wasn't true. The devil can't touch something as pure as Lyric. That was all God's doing. She is God's doing. Lyric was placed here for more than just me. She was put on this earth to guide others like Wendy. She's here to sing her heart out and bring happiness to all of those around her. Just knowing that brings tears to my eyes.

Sitting in the same spot I have for so many years, I pull my gun out of my jeans. I look at it as it sits heavily in my hand, taunting me. It's the same thing every year, except this year, I know I'm right. There isn't any more doubt. There isn't any reason to overthink it. Everything that has happened in my life has brought me to this one moment in time. As easily as I breathe the air in my lungs, I raise the gun to the side of my head, and say, "Happy birthday, Gabe."

Chapter 32

It's Lyric's big day. The day she stands in front of the crowd to sing her heart out. The guys all fill the front row, which makes me chuckle. I never thought that they would come. Hawk looks more nervous than Lyric. It's a little funny to be honest. Wendy sits proudly amongst them, which always brings a smile to my face. She has really taken to Lyric, and I think that's a good thing. Lyric paces around, her eyes focused on the crow tattoo on the top of her right hand. She runs her fingers over it again and again like it's a soothing thing. For her, I believe it is. She has the spirit of a fighter. If anyone can nail this, it's her. Lyric finally takes a deep breath before walking up to the microphone. Her hands shake slightly.

"You can do this, baby," I say softly as if she can hear me. When Lyric opens her mouth, her heart pours out. The crowd is on their feet much like I knew they would be. I learned over my time with her that her favorite band was Evanescence and that's the first song she ever sang at the clubhouse. This one is different. It's slower and deeper. It's her feelings coming out. It's every single emotion - the fear, hate, rage, and anger.

Even happiness comes through in her music. I
close my eyes as I listen to the words.

"I'm so tired of being here

Suppressed by all my childish fears

And if you have to leave

I wish that you would just leave

'Cause your presence still lingers here

And it won't leave me alone

*These wounds won't seem to heal, this pain
is just too real*

There's just too much that time cannot erase

*When you cried, I'd wipe away all of your
tears*

*When you'd scream, I'd fight away all of
your fears*

*And I held your hand through all of these
years*

But you still have all of me

*You used to captivate me by your resonating
light*

Now, I'm bound by the life you left behind

Your face, it haunts my once pleasant dreams

Your voice, it chased away all the sanity in me

These wounds won't seem to heal, this pain is just too real

There's just too much that time cannot erase."

The little tug on my hand causes me to pull away from the beauty of her song and open my eyes.

"You didn't have to come be with me, you know? You could have stayed with Lyric." I turn my head and look down at Gabe and the smile on his face. "I was okay watching you," he says.

I shake my head and lift him in my arms. My hearts at peace now more than ever. It's a feeling I never thought I'd have after I lost him. Now I have it again.

"No. Lyric needs to find her own way. I found mine, buddy. I need you more than you needed me. More than she needed me," I tell him being honest.

"She sings like an angel, Daddy," Gabe says as we look down at Lyric once more. That's because she is. She's my angel, much the way I am hers now.

"She does. Come on. Let's go." I smile as I take one last look at her on that stage pouring her heart out.

"Is Lyric gonna be okay, Daddy?"

"Yeah. She's just a little sad right now, but she's gonna be fine," I tell him sounding very sure of myself. I know she will. She promised me and Lyric doesn't break her promises. Besides, look at the family she has sitting in the front row to cheer her on. How could she not?

"Good. Cause I missed you, Daddy."

"Well, I'm here now and you never have to miss me again." I turn on my heel and walk into the breeze.

This is my happy ending. To some, it may seem wrong, but in my heart, I know it's right.

Did you enjoy Crow, Soulless Bastards MC? Keep in mind that this is just the So Cal Chapter's series. There will be more to come! Stick around and watch for the Florida Chapter's!

Like always, if you enjoyed this book please leave a review. Come stalk me on facebook at Erin M Trejo. Like my author page! Join my reader group, Fire and Ice.

14346447R00120

Printed in Germany
by Amazon Distribution
GmbH, Leipzig